Edmund B. Wilson

The DEVELOPMENT of RENILLA

Edmund B. Wilson

The DEVELOPMENT of RENILLA

ISBN/EAN: 9783741123436

Manufactured in Europe, USA, Canada, Australia, Japa

Cover: Foto ©Andreas Hilbeck / pixelio.de

Manufactured and distributed by brebook publishing software
(www.brebook.com)

Edmund B. Wilson

The DEVELOPMENT of RENILLA

THE DEVELOPMENT

OF

RENILLA.

BY

EDMUND B. WILSON, Ph.D.,

FELLOW OF JOHNS HOPKINS UNIVERSITY.

From the PHILOSOPHICAL TRANSACTIONS OF THE ROYAL SOCIETY.—Part III. 1883.

RENILLA.

𝔅. 𝔯athbun.

BY

EDMUND B. WILSON, Ph.D.,

FELLOW OF JOHNS HOPKINS UNIVERSITY.

From the PHILOSOPHICAL TRANSACTIONS OF THE ROYAL SOCIETY.—Part III. 1883.

XXIV. *The Development of Renilla.*

By Edmund B. Wilson, *Ph.D., Fellow of Johns Hopkins University.*

Communicated by Professor Huxley, *F.R.S.*

Received October 5,—Read December 14, 1882.

[Plates 52–67.]

The observations recorded in the following pages were made in the course of three summers' work at the marine laboratory of the Johns Hopkins University, organised and directed by Professor W. K. Brooks, and located for the past three years at Beaufort, N.C., where the material for this paper was collected.

The abundance of *Renilla reniformis* (Cuv.), at Beaufort, suggested the desirability of a careful study of its embryology, and this was rendered still more apparent by the studies which Mr. Mitsukuri had made upon the anatomy of the adult organism.

I was therefore much pleased when a lucky accident, during the summer of 1880, put me in possession of a few very young colonies. Subsequent search over the ground resulted in the discovery of a considerable number of young colonies in various stages of growth, and I was thus enabled to make a rather full study of the growth of the colony from the simple primary or axial polyp up to the adult organism with its secondary polyps in a state of full sexual maturity. A single specimen, finally, of the ciliated larva was taken at the surface and kept in the aquarium until the free-swimming life was abandoned and the characteristic tentacles and spicules made their appearance.

An outline of the general results of these observations was published in the American Journal of Science for December, 1880, a full description being however deferred in the hope of procuring still earlier stages for a study of the embryonic development. This hope was happily realised in the following summer, when two or three lots of fertilised eggs were obtained; and, finally, in the season of 1882, the eggs were procured in considerable abundance, and a very satisfactory study of the phenomena of development was effected.

During the latter season the eggs of a Gorgonian, *Leptogorgia virgulata* (Edw. and Haime), were procured—though in small numbers only—and I have studied to some extent the development of this polyp also. The material was however scanty, and the development, so far as observed, closely similar to that of *Renilla*; hence these observations will be described only for the sake of comparison and in connexion with those relating to *Renilla*.

I have been unable to overcome entirely certain technical difficulties, and my results will therefore be found inconclusive on a few points. Furthermore, the unexpected close of the spawning period during the last season's work brought to an unwelcome close my observations on the earlier stages of development, and I have not been able, for this reason, to follow in detail the phenomena of the fertilisation of the egg and the behaviour of the segmentation-nuclei during the early stages. Still I venture to hope that my observations form a decided advance on what is now known of the development of the Alcyonaria. KOWALEVSKY's well-known observations on *Sympodium*, *Clavularia*, *Alcyonium*, and *Gorgonia* form the basis of almost the whole of our knowledge of the subject; and these observations, though of great interest, were published in a very condensed form, and were in part rendered inaccessible to many zoologists through their publication in the Russian language. They indicated that the early stages of Alcyonarian polyps would well repay more extended observation, and this expectation has perhaps been realised in the case of *Renilla*.

So far as the Pennatulacea are concerned, nothing is known of the embryonic development, and only the most meagre accounts exist concerning the mode of budding and formation of the colony. The latter phenomena however involve questions of much interest on account of the highly specialised nature of the colony as expressed in the marked polymorphism of its members and in the remarkable relations of symmetry existing between them.

For the foregoing reasons it seems to me desirable to publish these observations without further delay, since I can see in the future no near opportunity of making them complete.

Before considering the phenomena of development it will be useful to glance for a moment at some of the structural features of the adult *Renilla* and their relation to the characteristics of other Alcyonaria. For a full description the reader is referred to the well-known papers of KÖLLIKER[*] and EISEN,[†] who have described in some detail the structure of *Renilla reniformis* and *R. amethystina*.

Renilla is a genus of Pennatulacea, a group which forms the highest division of the Order Alcyonaria. The organism, when adult, is a community or colony, the members of which consist of an axial polyp and a large number of secondary polyps produced by the budding of the axial or primary individual and organically united with it. The colony has the form of a reniform disc with a deep sinus at one side into which is inserted a flexible peduncle which roots the organism in the sand. The polyps are arranged in radiating lines over the surface, projecting upwards over the general

---

* "Anatomisch-Systematische Beschreibung der Alcyonarien, Erste Abtheilung, Die Pennatuliden." Abdruck a. d. Abhandlungen d. Senkenb. Naturforsch. Gesellschaft, Bd. vii., viii. Frankfort, 1872.

† "Bidrag til Kännedom om *Renilla*." Kongl. Svensk. Vet. Handl., Bd. xiii.

surface but lying nearly horizontally at the margin, where new polyps continually make their appearance. Each polyp may be retracted into a " cell " which is morphologically the basal part of the polyp and forms a part of the disc.

The polyp has eight septa or mesenteries, eight pinnate tentacles, and eight mesenterial or gastric filaments, of which the dorsal pair are more slender and of different structure from the others. The two lateral pairs of septa bear the reproductive organs, male or female, as the case may be, the sexes being separate. The septa are provided with delicate longitudinal muscles by which the retraction of the polyp into its cell is effected. These muscles are always placed on the ventral sides of the septa, so that the dorsal gastric chamber contains no muscles, while the ventral chamber contains them on both sides. Thus we observe a marked bilateral symmetry in the arrangement of all the internal organs, which is further emphasized in the dorso-ventral elongation of the mouth and œsophagus. This symmetry is expressed also in the arrangement of the calyx-teeth, which are conical projections from the walls of the gastric chambers at the level of the upper face of the disc. The ventral chamber is always destitute of a tooth, the dorsal chamber always bears one, and the lateral teeth are symmetrically arranged with respect to the dorso-ventral axis.

Besides the large sexual polyps there are other forms known as the *rudimentary individuals*, or in KÖLLIKER's terminology, as the *zooids*. These are microscopic in size, have no tentacles, no mesenterial filaments, no reproductive organs, and commonly only two calyx-teeth—those, namely, on the ventro-lateral chambers. The zooids possess, in fact, only septa, mouth, and œsophagus, the latter being richly ciliated within. Two distinct forms of zooids exist. One of these is represented by a single large zooid, placed near the middle of the disc on the dorsal side, and provided with the full number of calyx-teeth. It is for the most part through the mouth of this zooid that the water is discharged which circulates through the cavities of the colony. For this reason I shall call it the *exhalent zooid*, a name which seems preferable to KÖLLIKER's term " Haupt zooid." The other zooids are arranged in groups or clusters on the dorsal sides of the polyp-cells in the median line ; there are usually four such groups on each cell. It is their function to draw water from the exterior into the cavities of the colony, as may be shown by adding finely pulverised carmine to the water of the aquarium. Minute but powerful currents may thus be seen setting into the open mouths of the zooids. The zooids, like the sexual polyps, exhibit a marked bilateral symmetry in the disposition of all their organs ; the mouth and œsophagus are elongated in the dorso-ventral plane, the gastric chambers are of different sizes and symmetrical arrangement, and the two calyx-teeth occupy corresponding positions on the sides of the median plane.

The colony as a whole is also bilaterally symmetrical to a very striking degree. This is more obvious in young specimens, but is always clearly marked even in the largest colonies. Each polyp has its counterpart on the opposite side of the colony, and the dorso-ventral axes of the two polyps have the same inclination to that of the axial polyp, since the ventral chamber, which bears no calyx-teeth, is always directed outwards towards the margin of the disc. Thus the secondary polyps stand at all angles from 0° to 90° with the axial polyp ; those at the sides are placed so that their dorso-ventral axes form right angles with that of the axial polyp, while those directly in front of the axial polyp coincide with it in direction.

Lastly we may note the structure of the peduncle. Its cavity is divided into a dorsal and a ventral chamber by a horizontal partition which is pierced along its sides and at its lower extremity with openings by which the chambers are put in communication. Both chambers end blindly in front, but communicate by small openings with the adjacent polyp-cells. The upper canal communicates with the exterior through the exhalent zooid already described. The horizontal partition appears to split anteriorly into a dorsal and a ventral plate, between which lies the posterior part of the body— *i.e.*, part of the cell—of the axial polyp.

The structure of the body-wall in the peduncle, where it is most fully developed, is as follows (after EISEN). Beginning with the exterior there are : (1) external epithelium ; (2) a thick layer of connective tissue containing the spicules ; (3) a layer of fibrous connective tissue free from spicules ; (4) longitudinal muscles ; (5) circular muscles ; (6) internal epithelium. In other parts of the body the arrangement is somewhat different since the amount and structure of the connective tissue varies in different parts of the body and the spicules are absent from the walls of the free portions of the polyps.

Many of the structural features of *Renilla* are common to other Alcyonaria. The polyps always exhibit more or less of bilateral symmetry in the elongation of the mouth, disposition of the septa and septal muscles, grouping of the mesenterial filaments and arrangement of the reproductive organs. In all but one or two cases colonies are formed by processes of asexual multiplication, and these not uncommonly show traces of bilateral symmetry. Among the Pennatulacea bilaterality is always more or less marked, culminating in the *Renillaceæ*, where the symmetry is nearly complete.

The definite relation between the dorso-ventral axes of the secondary and primary polyps has been observed in a few other Alcyonaria, but observations on this point are very scanty. KÖLLIKER, in his great work on the Pennatulids, has described something similar among the more typical forms, and it is highly probable that further investigation would show that in all Pennatulacea definite relations of this sort exist. MOSELEY observed in *Heliopora* and *Sarcophyton*[*] that the dorsal sides of the polyps face in a definite direction ; and according to HAACKE[†] the polyps of *Madrepora* have a like disposition. As pointed out further on, this matter is one of much theoretical interest in connexion with the law of budding in *Renilla*.

* Phil. Trans., Vol. 166, 1876.
† " Zur Blastologie der Korallen," Jena. Zeitschrift, Bd. XIII

The polymorphism of the Pennatulids was first observed by VERRILL in 1864 in *Renilla*, and was afterwards shown by KÖLLIKER to be of general occurrence in the group. It occurs also in some of the Alcyonacea, as in *Sarcophyton* (MOSELEY) and *Heteroxenia* (KÖLLIKER), and Professor VERRILL has informed me of his discovery of rudimentary individuals in two species of *Paragorgia*, members of the Gorgonacea.

For our knowledge of the embryology of the Alcyonaria we are almost entirely indebted to KOWALEVSKY'S well-known researches, though LACAZE-DUTHIERS, many years earlier, made a few observations on the development of *Corallium*. In 1873 KOWALEVSKY gave some account of the embryological development of *Alcyonium digitatum* and *Gorgonia verrucosa*,* and in 1879 published a brief account of the early development of *Sympodium coralloides* and *Clavularia crassa*,† which he studied in conjunction with MARION. KÖLLIKER has given a brief account of the development of the buds in *Halisceptrum*, and DALYELL published fragmentary notes on the early development of *Virgularia*.‡

Even less is known in regard to the development of the colony in the Pennatulacea. FRITZ MÜLLER observed in 1864 the simple axial polyp of *Renilla* and gave a few notes upon its structure. KÖLLIKER figures a very young colony of *Pteroides* and gives a few notes concerning the young stages of *Kophobelemnon*. WILLEMÖES-SUHM has also described and figured one or two of the early stages of the colony in *Umbellularia*.§ A thorough study of the mode of budding has, however, never been made; and the observations just mentioned, though of interest, are too incomplete to be of great value.

In all of the Alcyonaria thus far studied the germ-layers appear to be differentiated through some process of delamination. Among other polyps, however—as we know from the observations of KOWALEVSKY, LACAZE-DUTHIERS, METSCHNIKOFF, JOURDAN and others—some forms undoubtedly pass through a typical invaginate gastrula stage, while others appear to develop as delaminate planulæ. BALFOUR states on the authority of KLEINENBERG,‖ that in a number of Zoantharia the segmentation is unequal, "indicating, perhaps, the occurrence of an epibolic gastrula." I shall, however, show further on, that inequality in cleavage is by no means a certain indication of epibolic invagination.

With this brief sketch of the anatomy and embryology of the Alcyonaria, in which

---

* "Untersuchungen über die Entwickelung der Cœlenteraten, Nachrichten der Kaiserl., Gesellsch. der Freunde der Naturkenntniss der Anthropologie und Ethnographie." Moskau, 1873 (Russian). Abstract in HOFFMANN and SCHWALBE's 'Jahresbericht,' 1875, Bd. ii.

† 'Zoologischer Anzeiger,' No. 38, 1879.

‡ 'Rare and Remarkable Animals of Scotland,' vol. ii., pp. 181–190, t. KÖLLIKER.

§ 'Annals and Magazine of Natural History,' vol. xv., 1875.

‖ 'Comparative Embryology,' vol. i.

5 A 2

only those features have been mentioned which appear of interest in connexion with the following study of *Renilla*, we may pass to a description of the observations.[*]

I.

SEGMENTATION OF THE EGG AND FORMATION OF THE GERMINAL LAYERS.

§ 1. *External features of segmentation.*

Renilla, like most other Alcyonaria, is diœcious, and on account of the rather marked difference in colour between the ova and spermatic capsules, the sexes may usually be distinguished by external examination. During the months of May, June, and July many *Renillas* were found with the cavities of the polyps packed with the lead-coloured ovaries or the whitish spermatic capsules. The egg or mass of sperm-cells is enclosed in a very distinct follicle of ciliated entoderm cells which is ruptured at the time of spawning, the eggs being thus discharged into the gastric cavity and thence passed out to the exterior.

The eggs make their exit through the mouths of the sexual polyps, and the time occupied in spawning is very short. They are vomited forth in great masses, together with a considerable quantity of mucus, by a reversed peristaltic movement of the œsophagus, the entire colony being usually in a state of complete expansion. The mass of eggs is often held for some time clasped in the tentacles before being thrown off into the water. All of the polyps in the central part of the disc spawn simultaneously; those near the edge of the disc often do not spawn with the others,

* It is perhaps worth while to describe briefly the methods employed in the preparation of the embryos. For sections of the early stages the most satisfactory method is that recommended by Bobretsky and so successfully employed by Mayer, Hatschek, and others. The eggs were heated in sea-water to about 60° C., and maintained at that temperature for two or three minutes in order to coagulate thoroughly the protoplasm. They were then hardened for twenty-four hours in potassium bichromate, washed two hours in sea-water, and then gradually hardened in alcohol (50 per cent. three hours, 75 per cent. three hours, 90 per cent. six hours, and then transferred to absolute alcohol). After standing twenty-four hours in picro-carmine, and again soaking a few hours in absolute alcohol, they were embedded in paraffin and vaseline and cut with the sledge microtome.

For sections of later stages the embryos were exposed for a few minutes to very dilute osmic acid (½⁰ per cent., or less) until a barely perceptible brown tint was produced. After thorough washing they were transferred to weak, strong and absolute alcohol, and stained and embedded as before.

For isolation of the muscle-fibres and other elements of the tissues, the method recommended by the Hertwig brothers was employed. The larvæ were placed for ten or fifteen minutes in a mixture of equal parts of ½⁰ per cent. osmic acid and ⅓ per cent. acetic acid in sea-water, then thoroughly washed and soaked for several days in ⅓ per cent. acetic acid in sea-water. They were then stained *in toto* and teased in glycerine.

With other methods of hardening I have had no success. Bobretsky's method is highly to be recommended for the early stages, and affords very clear and satisfactory preparations.

perhaps because they are younger and less mature. The ovaries of polyps which had recently spawned were usually found to contain considerable quantities of immature eggs. Hence it seems probable that there may be several successive broods of egg in a single year, since the spawning season extends over two or three months.

It is a rather curious fact that the eggs are always laid at very nearly the same hour of the day, viz., about 6 A.M. Large numbers of *Renillas* were kept in aquaria, and the act of spawning was several times observed. In a single case only the spawning took place as early as half-past five and it was never observed to occur later than 7 A.M. This regularity appears to be independent of temperature, although this has a very important influence on the rate of development; for the hour was the same on cold and warm days. It is not unlikely that marine animals are more regular in such habits than has been suspected. A similar case is that of *Lucifer*, which, as Dr. BROOKS has observed, deposits its eggs always at the same hour, viz. : from 9 to 10 P.M.

During the discharge of the eggs by the females the males pour out the spermatic fluid in a milky cloud rising from the colony. The male element is apparently discharged, like the eggs, through the mouths of the sexual polyps. The spermatozoa are of the ordinary tailed form with pyriform heads, and swim with great activity. Fertilisation is effected in the water.

When first discharged the eggs are usually more or less distorted by pressure during their passage through the œsophagus; within a few minutes, however, they become perfectly spherical, and have an average diameter of about ·35 mm. They are of stony opacity, so that the germinal vesicle is invisible, and are destitute of any proper limiting membrane, though the peripheral layer of the vitellus is clearer and less granular than the rest. The entire substance of the vitellus is densely packed with deutoplasm granules, which upon rupture of the egg appear as clear yellowish spherules. Polar cells were never observed.

It will be convenient to describe first those changes which are visible from the exterior, leaving to the next section an account of the corresponding internal changes as discovered in sections. In a third section a review of the facts will be given, together with a discussion of their significance.

The segmentation of the egg in *Renilla* is remarkable for the surprising amount of individual variation of which it is capable. So great is this variation that it is safe to say that no two eggs ever develop in precisely the same way; and although most of the variations may be arranged in a definite series, some of them are so irregular that they seem to follow no definite law. No one indeed without actually following the entire development of some of these eggs would suppose them capable of normal development. For a long time, in fact, I passed by some of the less usual forms as due to abnormal or pathological changes, and only after repeated and careful study was able to convince myself that these peculiar embryos gave rise to active larvæ, differing in no visible respect from those which had developed along the more usual course. The matter appeared to me of such interest and importance that I gladly availed myself of the aid of two of my fellow workers at the laboratory—Mr. H. L. OSBORN and Dr. J. MEREDITH WILSON—in order to study as completely as possible the various forms of development. A large number of eggs, produced at different times by different individuals, were kept under continuous observation from the time of fertilisation up to an advanced stage of the segmentation ; they were then proved to be capable of full and normal development by isolation in small glass vessels until the free-swimming larval stage was attained. We were thus enabled to determine with all possible certainty the fact that at least five or six well-marked modes of yolk-cleavage, with many minor variations, may occur as normal phenomena of development, that the segmentation may be at first equal or unequal, complete or partial, regular or irregular, and that a great amount of variation exists in the duration of the various stages of activity and quiescence.

The interval between fertilisation and the first cleavage varies greatly, and is in general greater when the temperature is low. Segmentation may begin within ninety minutes after fertilisation, or it may be delayed three or four hours beyond this. It was found that the longer this preliminary quiescence continued, the more apt the eggs were to pass through the less usual modes of development, while those which developed promptly were as a rule of the two common types about to be described.

1. I will first describe a common, though not the most frequent, mode of development illustrated by figs. 1 to 18. The egg having remained perfectly spherical from the time of fertilisation, becomes of irregular outline, and in two or three minutes divides into eight equal segmentation spheres. These are at first imperfectly separated (fig. 1), but soon become exceedingly distinct (fig. 2). In the individual figured the spheres swelled up slightly one minute later (fig. 3), then gradually flattened together somewhat, and the egg passed into a slightly-marked quiescent period or "resting stage" (figs. 4, 5). This continued fifteen minutes, when the spheres again swelled up, and each divided into equal parts (fig. 6) so that the embryo consisted of sixteen spheres. These again flattened together somewhat, and a second resting stage ensued (fig. 7) which continued for twenty minutes. The slight swelling of the spheres shown in fig. 3 is not accompanied by any visible cleavage. It is probably attendant upon some internal change, which may, perhaps, be a division of the nuclei —possibly of the spheres also—in a plane parallel with the surface. It is certain that such cleavages take place sooner or later, but I have not been able to trace the connexion between them and the external signs of activity (see § 2).

The segmentation now proceeded with great regularity, and appeared from the exterior to be regular and complete. Each stage of division, during which the spheres are swollen and rounded, was followed by a period of quiescence, in which the spheres were flattened and more closely pressed together. This regular alternation of rest and activity continued for a long time, until the spheres had become very small and the embryo had begun to elongate. It is clearly shown in the series of figures from 1 to 18, of which the first fourteen are from one individual (time, 115 minutes), the last four from another specimen (time, 32 minutes). The intervals of time between the successive visible cleavages were somewhat irregular, as shown in the following statement :—

Between figures	2 and 5 .	9 minutes.
„	5 „ 7 .	45 „
„	7 „ 9 .	29 „
„	9 „ 11 .	12 „
„	11 „ 13 .	23 „
„	13 „ 15 .	Not observed.
„	15 „ 17 . .	27 minutes.

In the eggs of many animals the periods follow one another with great uniformity, and the irregularity in the present case is therefore somewhat unusual. It depends perhaps on the fact that the embryo is solid, and that during the whole segmentation the cleavages take place not only in planes at right angles to the surface, but also in planes parallel to it. The latter cleavages would not be visible externally, but might retard the surface cleavages at certain periods. This is apparently the true explanation of the long delay of forty-five minutes between figs. 5 and 7 ; for, as we shall see in the following section, the delamination, by means of which the layers are separated, takes place at this period when the embryo consists of sixteen spheres.

2. The mode of segmentation which has been described occurred with slight variations in rather less than one-third of all the eggs studied. In the most usual case, however, the eight-sphere stage is entirely passed over, and the egg divides at once into sixteen spheres at the first cleavage.

This mode of cleavage, illustrated by figs. 30 to 37, is, except in the first stage, quite like the cleavage into eight spheres. The egg is at first perfectly spherical, then becomes irregular in form, with a wavy outline, and at length falls at once into sixteen spheres (fig. 33), which are, as a rule, of equal size. Though very distinct at first, they soon flatten together, and the egg passes into a resting stage (fig. 35), which continues for ten to twenty minutes. This quiescent period, though only slightly marked in the specimen figured, is sometimes very pronounced, so that the embryo may be nearly or quite indistinguishable from the unsegmented egg. The subsequent development is very regular, and is like the first case.

As noted above, the spheres are usually of equal size. It is, however, a common occurrence for the segmentation to be more or less unequal, as shown in figs. 38 to 44. In this case the embryo presents externally the appearance of an epibolic gastrula, consisting of macromeres and micromeres. In the eight-sphere stage, also, embryos were sometimes observed to consist of four large spheres, capped by smaller ones, exactly as in the early stages of many epibolic gastrulas. In the sixteen-sphere stage there are often three or four larger spheres which are always placed at one pole of the egg, and are not separated by smaller spheres.

The first cleavage into eight spheres may be incomplete and irregular as well as unequal. Thus the egg shown in figs. 45 to 48 divided at first incompletely into eight (fig. 45), and then passed into a somewhat marked quiescent stage (fig. 46) of fifteen minutes' duration, one of the spheres retaining its prominence, as shown in the figure. It then divided into sixteen nearly equal spheres (figs. 47, 48), and its subsequent development was regular. A somewhat similar case is illustrated by figs. 49 to 58. In this individual the first resting stage (figs. 51, 52) was very marked, the outlines of the spheres became quite invisible, and the embryo could only be distinguished from the unsegmented egg by its slightly irregular outline. In this individual it is shown, further, that the spheres do not necessarily divide simultaneously, though this is usually the case. The sphere marked a. did not divide at the third general cleavage (fig. 55), but delayed until the next, or fourth, cleavage, when it divided into two spheres, a.a.

In these cases of slightly unequal cleavage it was in several instances observed that the smaller spheres sometimes increased considerably in size, after the cleavage was apparently complete, so as to reduce the inequality considerably. This is rendered possible, perhaps, by the circumstance to be afterwards described, that the earlier cleavages do not extend to the middle of the ovum, and the spheres are continuous at first with a central solid unsegmented mass. Or it may possibly be due to a re-arrangement of the material of the spheres, such as a change from a vertical to a horizontal elongation.

3. In the third form of segmentation to be described, of which a single case only was observed by Dr. WILSON, the egg divided at the first visible cleavage into thirty-two ($\pm$) spheres, passing over both the eight-sphere and the sixteen-sphere stages. The segmentation was somewhat unequal and became more so in later stages owing to the more rapid multiplication of the spheres at one pole. The egg developed perfectly, however, and produced a larva which appeared to be quite normal.

In the three forms of segmentation so far described, a certain number of individuals were observed to undergo considerable changes of form fifteen to twenty-five minutes before actual cleavage took place. The eggs became slightly irregular, with wavy outlines, as if about to segment; but within a few minutes they became again perfectly spherical, and remained so until the actual segmentation began. This was observed only once preliminary to the eight-sphere cleavage, and occurred in the single example of the thirty-two-sphere division. About one-fourth of those which divided at once into sixteen underwent the preliminary change.

There can be little doubt that these preliminary changes of form are attendant upon divisions of the nuclei. The egg appears to make an effort, so to speak, at cleavage, but has not sufficient energy to complete the division of the vitellus. I shall return to this point further on. It is perhaps worth noting that the interval (fifteen to twenty-five minutes) between the preliminary change and the first cleavage is nearly always considerably greater than the ordinary resting stages (eight to eighteen minutes).

4. In a fourth form of segmentation (figs. 19 to 24), of which a single example only was observed, the egg was divided at first into two equal parts by a horizontal cleavage, and then incompletely into eight by two partial vertical furrows at right angles to each other and to the horizontal furrows (figs. 19, 20). The vertical furrows started from the horizontal one at four equi-distant points, and travelled about half-way towards the upper and lower poles. They stopped abruptly at these points however, and the egg passed into a very marked resting stage (fig. 21), during which the form was nearly spherical and the furrows could only be seen at the points of union with each other. At the next cleavage the egg divided into about sixteen spheres of different sizes (see fig. 22). The spheres remained sharply marked and rounded for twelve minutes, then flattened together slightly, but five minutes later swelled slightly and each divided into two with beautiful regularity (fig. 24). The subsequent development was regular and normal.

5. In one case an egg was observed to divide into two nearly equal parts, and then passed into a marked resting stage (figs. 25–27). In several other cases eggs were observed divided into four equal parts (figs. 28 and 29). Unluckily, the subsequent development was not followed in either case, and I cannot state whether these eggs were normal. In any case they are interesting, as filling out the series of different modes of segmentation of which the eggs are capable. In view of the great variation which certainly does exist it seems not improbable that these forms are capable of normal development.

6. In the cases so far described, the entire mass of the vitellus segments at the same time or nearly so. In several instances, however, segmentation began at one pole of the egg, leaving a large mass undivided at the opposite pole. These eggs had exactly the appearance of undergoing a partial segmentation, like that of *Pyrosoma*, or some Teleostean fishes. Thus in the egg shown by figs. 59 to 62 segmentation began with the formation of four small spheres at one pole of the egg, which then passed into a very marked resting stage. At the next cleavage (figs. 61, 62) the unsegmented portion broke up into about twelve spheres, of which two or three were somewhat larger than the others (fig. 62). The egg is now closely similar to that shown in fig. 38 which was directly derived from the unsegmented egg, and its subsequent development calls for no remark. Figs. 63 to 67 represent a similar case. In this instance the

small spheres at the second cleavage gradually extended downwards, being successively constricted off from the unsegmented mass. The first resting stage (fig. 64) was much less marked than in the individual last described, and in some individuals of this type the first period of quiescence is not attended by any flattening of the spheres, though a considerable pause always follows the formation of the first four or five small spheres.

7. Lastly, I may describe a very peculiar segmentation, shown by figs. 68 to 72. The egg when first observed consisted of three large spheres and four much smaller ones. One of the latter soon divided, and the egg passed into a slightly marked resting stage (fig. 70). At the next cleavage both large and small spheres divided (figs. 71 and 72) without apparent regularity, and the inequality still remained marked. In later stages the spheres gradually became more uniform in size, the embryo developed normally, and on the following day the free-swimming larva could not be distinguished from those produced by more usual forms of development.

Review.

The egg may divide at the first cleavage into two, four (?), eight, sixteen, or thirty-two spheres, which may be equal or unequal in size. In some cases the egg undergoes a preliminary change of form some time before cleavage, without, however, dividing, and returning afterwards to a spherical form. The cleavage into eight parts may be irregular and incomplete, and at the next cleavage sixteen spheres are formed.

Cleavage may begin at one pole of the egg with the formation of four or five small spheres, and (usually) after a quiescent period the remainder of the vitellus breaks up at once or progressively into spheres of approximately the same size as those first formed, and the egg passes into the sixteen-sphere stage.

Lastly, the segmentation may be very irregular as well as very unequal, and follows no discernible order.

I have described the various forms of segmentation in what may seem wearisome detail, since the existence of so wide a range of variation in segmentation is quite unprecedented, so far as recorded observations show. In the eggs of many animals the course of the segmentation appears to be remarkably constant, and the various cleavages follow one another with almost mathematical regularity. So far as I am aware, BROOKS was the first to point out, in the case of the Oyster, in 1879, that the eggs of the same species, or even of the same individual, may normally undergo more than one mode of development. He described in the Oyster two forms of segmentation, of which one was clearly derived by an abbreviation of the other. Intermediate forms were not, however, observed, and the eggs could not be said to exhibit variation except in one definite direction. In *Renilla* the eggs vary in many directions, and the different forms of development must be due to varying structural arrangements within the egg.

This fact of extremely early variation is, I believe, one of great importance. It is evident that a structural variation in one of the segmentation spheres must make itself felt, to a greater or less extent, in the structure and development of the cells derived from it, and may therefore appear ultimately as symmetrical or correlated variations in the larva or adult organism.

Leptogorgia, like *Renilla*, is diœcious, and the eggs are fertilised in the water after their discharge from the parent. The eggs are slightly smaller (·30 millim.), and of a rosy tint, but are otherwise quite similar to those of *Renilla*. They are discharged in the same manner through the mouths of the polyps, and at the same hour of the day, viz., 6 A.M. Unlike *Renilla*, the eggs are discharged in small numbers only, each polyp producing, so far as could be ascertained, only two or three ripe eggs at a time. The polyps in all parts of the colony discharge their eggs nearly simultaneously.

The segmentation is closely similar to the most common mode of *Renilla*, but differs in some rather interesting particulars. Owing perhaps to the scarcity of material, variations in the segmentation were not observed; but only three or four eggs were kept under continuous observation from the time of fertilisation. In all these cases the egg underwent slight changes of form about an hour before the beginning of segmentation, returning afterwards to an almost perfectly spherical form. The interval between this change of form (which is undoubtedly, as in *Renilla*, the expression of an attempt at cleavage) and the beginning of actual segmentation is much greater than in *Renilla*.

At the first cleavage the egg divides into sixteen very distinct equal spheres, which soon flatten together very completely, and a strongly marked quiescent period follows, during which the embryo can scarcely be distinguished from the unsegmented egg. This continues for about twenty minutes, when the spheres again swell up and become very distinct but *do not divide*. This condition continues for several minutes when the spheres again flatten down, and a second resting stage occurs which is rather less marked than the first.

Unluckily, I did not succeed in procuring satisfactory sections of this stage, since the methods of hardening employed with *Renilla* proved useless for *Leptogorgia*. There is every reason to believe, however, reasoning from analogy, that this swelling of the spheres is accompanied by a division of their substance; and this division can only be in a plane parallel with the surface—in other words, it must be a delamination cleavage. The delamination in *Renilla*, as we shall see, takes place when the embryo consists of sixteen segmentation spheres, but with considerable irregularity, and I have not been able to connect it certainly with any external sign of activity. In *Leptogorgia* all of the spheres appear to divide at nearly the same moment, the delamination being nearly as regular as in *Gorgonia* or *Liriope*.

The egg shown in figs. 73 to 106 developed nearly in the manner just described, but with the important difference that the delamination cleavage appeared to take place when the embryo consisted of thirty-two ($\pm$) instead of sixteen spheres. When first observed the egg consisted of thirty-two ($\pm$) spheres (fig. 73), which afterwards flattened together very completely (fig. 74). Fifteen minutes later the spheres swelled up and became very prominent (fig. 75), but the embryo passed into another quiescent stage (fig. 76) without visible division of the spheres.

Hence it would seem that the period at which delamination occurs is not invariable, or it may be that it takes place at different periods in different parts of the same egg. The number of eggs observed was not large enough to determine this interesting and important point.

The remainder of the segmentation (figs. 77 to 85) is closely similar to *Renilla* and does not call for special remark. . The periods of activity and quiescence alternate with great regularity, and have approximately the same duration as in *Renilla*. Although I have examined a considerable number of eggs (probably fifty or sixty), they were never found to consist of less than sixteen spheres or undergoing "partial" segmentation ; and although some inequality was observed, this was never so marked as in *Renilla*. It would therefore seem that the form of segmentation is more firmly fixed than in *Renilla*.

§ 2. *Internal phenomena of segmentation.*

a. The unsegmented egg.

In the fresh state no trace of a germinal vesicle can be seen in the unsegmented egg. A series of sections shows, however, that a large vesicle is present (fig. 86) containing a very distinct germinal spot. In immature eggs the vesicle lies near the centre of the egg, but in the ripe egg it is situated near the periphery of the vitellus. It is enclosed in a delicate but very distinct membrane, and has a somewhat reniform shape with the concave side turned outwards. The interior appears to be filled with a finely granular substance, which stains intensely. No protoplasmic reticulum can be seen, and if present its meshes must be of exceeding fineness so as to produce the appearance of a fine granulation. The germinal spot is of a rounded form and lies near the centre of the germinal vesicle. It is of high refrangibility and stains intensely with picro-carmine. Under a high magnifying power it is seen to consist of a lighter clear peripheral layer, enclosing a number of spheroidal bodies, which are separated by a reticulum of deeply staining substance.

The body of the vitellus consists of a fine protoplasmic network, closely packed with rounded granules of deutoplasm, which are scarcely affected by the staining fluid. A rather narrow peripheral zone of the vitellus does not take the staining fluid, and is of a more finely granular structure than the rest of the vitellus. This zone is faintly visible in fresh eggs when flattened under the compressor, and it persists until a late stage of the segmentation. In some preparations, however, it does not appear, and sometimes it is marked in one part of a section and invisible in other parts (see fig. 94).

As shown in fig. 86, the germinal vesicle lies in contact with this clear peripheral layer, which extends inwards slightly to meet it. In the section following that which is figured, the peripheral layer actually bends inwards so as to form a slight funnel-shaped depression leading inwards towards the germinal vesicle. Possibly this may be due to shrinkage; for I have never observed such a depression in fresh eggs. More probably it should be regarded as a kind of micropyle through which the spermatozöon enters the egg. The metamorphosis of the germinal vesicle, consequent upon fertilisation, was not followed.

As already stated, there is a considerable interval between fertilisation and the first visible cleavage. Sections through the egg show that, although the vitellus is apparently inactive, the nuclei are rapidly multiplying. The egg, which at first contains a single nucleus, becomes polynuclear and passes into the condition of a polyplast or syncytium, each nucleus corresponding to one of the future segmentation spheres, as shown by later sections.

I did not succeed in following completely the progressive multiplication of the nuclei, and can only assert that they become more numerous up to the time of cleavage, when each sphere contains a single nucleus. Many sections were obtained containing two nuclei, several with three, and a few in which four nuclei were visible. By making series of consecutive sections through the ova, it is possible to determine approximately the number of nuclei. I have thus observed the egg with four nuclei, others with four amphiasters, representing the multiplication of four nuclei into eight, and others containing eight separate nuclei. In others the number of nuclei is still greater, and in one case I was able to count sixteen nuclei, as described below. The nuclei do not always divide simultaneously, for I have, in several cases, observed eggs containing ordinary nuclei, and also typical amphiasters, with their characteristic spindles and star-shaped heads. In some cases an amphiaster and an undivided nucleus appear in the same section. In all these cases the eggs were perfectly spherical before treatment with reagents, and showed no sign of division.

Fig. 87 represents a section through a spherical unsegmented egg, a few minutes before its fellows divided into sixteen spheres. The irregularity of form is a result of shrinkage which, however, affects only the external form, leaving the substance of the vitellus uniform, and quite free from shrinkage cavities. This section is from one side of the egg, and contains two distinct amphiasters. Passing inwards, the second section contains two nuclei, and the third one. Four nuclei appear in the fourth, and four in the fifth, which is represented in fig. 88. Three of the latter are simple, while the fourth is elongated, and apparently about to become an amphiaster. Two nuclei appear in the sixth section, one in the seventh, one in the eighth, and a single amphiaster in the ninth and last. The four nuclei of sections 4 and 5 have the same relative positions, and are doubtless identical : the nucleus of No. 3 corresponds with one of No. 2 ; and one of No. 6 with that of No. 7. I find, counting each amphiaster as two nuclei, the egg contains fifteen nuclei, and, counting the elongating nucleus of No. 5 as two, we have a total of sixteen nuclei, corresponding with the number of spheres formed at the first cleavage.

The segmentation nuclei bear no resemblance to the germinal vesicle or egg-nucleus. When in the quiescent state they appear as intensely stained finely granular areas, shading off, insensibly, into the surrounding mass of the vitellus, and without enclosing membrane or nucleoli. In later stages, when the vitellus has undergone division, they sometimes appear as small vesicles, containing a clear substance, and a very deeply stained nucleolus. The yolk-granules are almost always disposed in radiating lines about the nucleus, but this appearance varies greatly, and is sometimes scarcely discernible. I have no new observations to offer on the phenomena attending their multiplication, since the abundance of deutoplasm obscures the structure of the nuclei and amphiasters. Nuclei were, however, observed in every stage of division, and I will briefly describe their transformation : The nucleus becomes slightly elongated, then decidedly so, and the radiate arrangement of the surrounding granules is very marked (fig 88). In a slightly later stage, the nucleus has a dumb-bell shape, with the vitelline granules radiating from each extremity Still later, the typical amphiaster form is attained, with two deeply stained nuclear areas, surrounded by very marked radiating lines of granules, and connected by a striated spindle. The stars then move apart, the spindle becomes attenuated. In later stages, during the cleavage process, the body of the cell splits into two at this stage of the amphiaster, the line of division passing at right angles to the spindle, near its middle point. In the unsegmented egg, the two stars simply move apart, and the spindle entirely disappears.

After the division of the amphiaster is completed, the two new nuclei assume the ordinary appearance, and the radiating arrangement of the yolk-granules becomes less marked.

The nuclei are at first situated near the centre of the egg, but as the time for cleavage approaches they travel towards the periphery, where the first segmentation spheres are to make their appearance,

b. The cleavage process.

The first division of the vitellus (fig. 89) consists in the formation of rounded prominences over its surface, of which each contains one of the nuclei derived from the continued division of the segmentation nucleus, and is therefore the equivalent of a cell (*i.e.*, a segmentation sphere). These spheres are however entirely fused together, and there is at first no trace of lines of division between them. The egg is still a polyplast or syncytium though the vitellus is being acted upon by forces which tend to split it up into separate portions corresponding in number with the nuclei. It is important to note that whether eight or sixteen spheres are formed at the first cleavage, each contains a single nucleus only ; for this shows that division of the vitellus does not always occur at the same stage in the division of the nuclei.

The prominences soon become very marked, increasing in size at the expense of the central mass and becoming at length of a pyriform shape. The egg then consists of a central unsegmented mass containing no nuclei, and surrounded by partly formed spheres, each containing a single nucleus and connected by a broad isthmus with the central mass. In some cases, at any rate, the embryo now passes into a resting stage, as shown in fig. 95. The spheres flatten together and are separated by very distinct narrow clear spaces, which terminate abruptly some distance from the centre, thus leaving the central mass quite unsegmented, and continuous with the mass of the partially-formed spheres. In the figure some of the spheres appear to be completely separated from the central mass, and this may perhaps be the case with some of them. Others however are certainly not separated from the central mass.

In the second stage of activity, or perhaps in some cases in the first, the spheres increase still further at the expense of the central mass, which becomes at length reduced to a very small remnant (fig. 92), to which the spheres are attached by narrow necks. Finally even this remnant disappears, and the completely formed spheres extend to the very centre of the embryo. A small mass of granular matter still remains in the middle of the embryo, and the spheres are attenuated at their inner ends (fig. 93). No segmentation cavity exists at this stage, but the inner ends of the cells soon become evenly rounded and a small segmentation cavity is formed (fig. 94), in which a quantity of granular *débris* usually remains. The spheres are destitute of cell-membranes, but are separated by a small quantity of intercellular substance. Their substance is completely similar to that of the unsegmented egg, the nuclei have the same appearance as in the latter, and are situated in the outer halves of the cells. The clear peripheral zone observed in the unsegmented egg is still very distinct in some specimens, but in others cannot be seen. It does not follow the lines of cleavage into the interior of the egg.

c. Formation of the layers.

The egg is now in the condition of a blastula in which the cells are not yet differentiated into ectoderm and entoderm. In the next change—which constitutes perhaps the most important epoch in the development of the larva—the ectoderm and entoderm are separated by a process of delamination ; *i.e.*, the inner end of each sphere separates as an entoderm cell from the outer portion which remains as an ectoderm cell. A careful study of my sections taken in connexion with the external appearances, leaves no room for doubt that this is the mode in which the layers are separated ; but it is clear that the cells do not in all cases perform the delamination cleavage simultaneously. On the contrary there appears to be much irregularity in this process, which is not surprising in view of the other remarkable variations in the segmentation which have been described. Thus, in the same specimen, some of the cells may be undivided and contain simple nuclei; others contain delamination amphiasters (*i.e.*, those whose long axes are radially directed); while others have completely divided into ectodermic and entodermic moieties. Moreover, delamination cleavages may be in progress in some of the cells, while in others the cleavages are taking place in vertical planes. This is shown, for instance, in fig. 99, where two of the cells (*a*, *b*) contain delamination amphiasters, as shown by the direction of their long axes, while a third cell (*c*) is about to divide in a vertical (or radial) plane, as shown by the position of the amphiaster.

This suggests the interesting question as to whether delamination cleavages really take place in all of the cells, or may not rather be limited to the cells over a certain area. My sections are inconclusive on this point, which is of great importance in its bearing on the mode of transition between the invaginate and delaminate modes of development. (See BALFOUR's 'Comparative Embryology,' vol. ii., p. 280, and my paper on the early stages of some polychætous annelides in 'Studies from the Biological Laboratory of the Johns Hopkins University,' vol. ii., No. 2, 1882; compare also the very interesting observations of CLAUS on "Die Entwickelung des Aequoriden-Eies," Zool. Anzeiger, No. 112, June, 1882.)

In fig. 94 one of the cells (*a*.) is in the act of cleavage, and the direction of the amphiaster and the form of the cell indicate that the cleavage is in a horizontal plane—*i.e.*, is a delamination cleavage. Fig. 96 represents a section (osmic acid) through an egg, a little later, in which the inner portions of several of the spheres are separating, or have recently separated, as entoderm cells. Unluckily, the nuclei do not appear in the section, which is furthermore somewhat disfigured by shrinkage cavities.

In a few cases I have observed at a much earlier period divisions of the nuclei, which may possibly represent delamination cleavages. Such a case is shown in fig. 98. The egg is about to divide into sixteen spheres, but contains two amphiasters, which have the same position as the true delamination amphiasters already described. It seems possible that the inner star of each amphiaster is destined to form the nucleus of an entoderm cell, and the outer star that of an ectoderm cell when division of the vitellus takes place. I have not traced this out, however, and the appearance may be open to a quite different interpretation. It is, however, certain that there is a good deal of variation in the delamination process, and the embryos do not display the beautiful regularity in this respect which has been described in some Cœlenterate eggs. As already mentioned, *Leptogorgia* appears to differ from *Renilla* in this respect, since the period of delamination is sufficiently marked to produce a special "active stage," represented externally by the simultaneous swelling of all the spheres.

At the close of the delamination process, the egg consists of a solid mass of cells in which every trace of the segmentation cavity has disappeared. As shown in figs. 99 and 100, the ectoderm does not at first form a distinct layer, the cells dovetailing with those of the central entodermic mass. As the egg passes into the resting stage, however (fig. 97), the ectoderm becomes pretty well defined as a single layer of large cuboidal cells. The central mass is composed of large rounded polygonal entoderm cells, which differ little in structure from those of the ectoderm.

§ 3. *General considerations and comparison with other forms.*

With the formation of the germ-layers the segmentation may be regarded as finished, and it may be useful to review the facts in comparison with other forms, in order to appreciate their significance.

Examples of the continued division of the segmentation nucleus before cleavage of the vitellus are very common, but in most cases the nuclei become far more numerous before cleavage occurs than in the ovum of *Renilla*. In the case of the Isopod *Asellus* (VAN BENEDEN) the segmentation is entirely similar to one of the forms observed in *Renilla*, the nuclei multiplying to the number of eight, and the vitellus then dividing at once into eight spheres. In view of the total dissimilarity of the adult forms, this identity in segmentation is a striking instance of the independence of the yolk-cleavage from the adult structure; and it would be clear, from this case alone, that the particular form of the segmentation may be wholly determined by secondary or adaptive causes.

This fact is rendered especially conspicuous from the astonishing amount of variation shown in the *Renilla* segmentation. This variation concerns not only small details, but also features which are usually held to be characteristic of quite different types of development. Hence we can see how readily the form of segmentation might be acted on by natural selection, for advantageous variations would certainly tend to be preserved and harmful ones destroyed. It must, however, be admitted that the action of heredity appears to have little precision in this case, for the most unlike variations appear in the eggs of the same parent, and I have not observed that any particular variation occurs more frequently in the eggs of particular individuals.

We may now inquire, What is the direct cause of the variations in the yolk-cleavage? As we have seen, the nuclei divide, so far as can be determined, in the ordinary course, and sooner or later the vitellus follows. It is highly probable that the division of the nuclei is in all cases nearly regular, and the variations of the yolk-cleavage depend upon the varying activity of the vitellus, either as a whole or in its various parts. There seems to be always a tendency to the cleavage of the vitellus simultaneously with the division of the nuclei, but this tendency varies in force or meets with varying resistance. As described above, the vitellus seems sometimes to make abortive attempts to divide simultaneously with the nuclei, these efforts being expressed in temporary changes of form in the vitellus, but not resulting in complete cleavages. In other cases the attempt is partially successful, as where the vitellus divides incompletely into eight (fig. 45). Sooner or later the tendency gathers energy enough to carry out a complete segmentation. The egg may be able to do this at the first division of the segmentation nucleus into two, or may be unable to effect it until six successive divisions of the nuclei have taken place, and the egg therefore divides into thirty-two spheres at the first cleavage.

In searching for the cause of these variations in the activity of the vitellus, the idea at once suggests itself that it lies in the variations of the amount and distribution of the deutoplasm. It has been pretty clearly established by the researches of late years that the protoplasmic and deutoplasmic constituents of the vitellus are, in a certain sense, antagonistic to each other in their influence upon the rate of development. The protoplasm is the active part, while the deutoplasm, *as such*, is inert, and, until absorbed and converted into protoplasm, exercises a retarding influence upon development.

The egg of *Renilla* is heavily laden with deutoplasm spheres, which, as we shall see, long remain inert, and are not converted into protoplasm until a late stage of development. If we suppose—and the assumption appears fully justifiable—that the amount and distribution of the deutoplasm in the vitellus are subject to slight variation, most of the variation receives a simple explanation. It is, of course, possible, or even probable, that the activity of the protoplasm may vary also ; but since the two constituents of the vitellus are, as it were, counterbalanced against each other, a variation in the amount or activity of the protoplasm must have the same effect as the opposite variation in the deutoplasm, and hence we may for the sake of simplicity consider the amount of deutoplasm alone.

The researches of FLEMMING, STRASBURGER, and others have within a few years clearly shown that the division of the nucleus of a cell produces, or is at any rate closely associated with, a tendency to division in the body of the cell. If then the deutoplasm of an egg be scanty, this tendency may be strong enough at the first division of the nucleus to overcome the inertia of the mass of the vitellus and the egg divides into two cleavage spheres at the start. This condition is permanently retained in the eggs of many animals, but in *Renilla* occurs only as a rare variation. With an increasing amount of deutoplasm, equally distributed, the cleavage of the vitellus is longer and longer delayed, though the ineffectual efforts of the vitellus may be expressed in slight changes in the form of the ovum.

Bearing these considerations in mind it is exceedingly interesting to compare the various modes of development of *Renilla* with those of other animals, and especially of certain forms existing among the Arthropods.

In *Lucifer*, as described by BROOKS (Phil. Trans., 1882), the egg is transparent and nearly destitute of deutoplasm. The segmentation is regular and total, the nuclei and bodies of the spheres divide regularly and simultaneously into two, four, eight, &c., as far as the segmentation can be followed, and the spheres remain perfectly distinct from one another. In *Palæmon*, described by BOBRETSKY (whose Russian paper I know only from German abstracts), the deutoplasm is abundant, but the segmentation is regular and total at first. Late in the development, however, the inner ends of the high columnar cells (" yolk pyramids ") fuse together to form a homogeneous yolk. *Penæus* (HAECKEL) undergoes a similar development, but the fusion of the inner ends of the spheres occurs at a far earlier stage when only four spheres are formed. Whether these are at first distinct was not determined.

In *Eupagurus* and a number of other Decapods studied by MAYER (Jenaische Zeitschrift, Bd. xi., 1877) a curious condition exists which is intermediate between the preceding forms and *Renilla*. The nucleus divides regularly into two, four, and eight, but without a concomitant cleavage of the vitellus. After the formation of the eight nuclei, however, the vitellus divides into two, four, and eight complete spheres, each of which contains one of the nuclei. In the next stage sixteen spheres are formed, but their inner ends no longer extend to the middle of the egg, the spheres having fused to form a yolk-mass as in *Penæus* or *Palæmon*. Finally in *Asellus*, already referred to, the nuclei multiply as in *Eupagurus* to the number of eight, but the vitellus then divides *at once* into eight partially-formed spheres, without undergoing the previous divisions into two and four. This condition is characteristic of about one-third of the *Renilla* eggs, but in most cases the division of the vitellus is retarded until sixteen nuclei are formed.

In rare cases cleavage is delayed until thirty-two nuclei are formed, and here again we find that this condition, though a rare variation in *Renilla*, is permanent and normal in another group of animals, namely, the Araneina (HUB. LUDWIG, Zeitsch. Wiss. Zool., Bd. xxvi., 1876). In this well known case the nuclei multiply to the number of thirty-two before the vitellus actually divides, though a partial segregation of its material is effected. From this condition the step is not great to the eggs of the Insecta and Acarina, where a still larger number of nuclei are formed before cleavage begins.

There can be no doubt that the regular division of the vitellus in geometrical progression into two, four, &c., spheres, is in general to be regarded as the most primitive mode of development, the process being only a special case of cell-division. In a number of polyps, both of the Alcyonarian and Actinarian types, as in *Clavularia*, or some species of *Actinia* (KOWALEVSKY), this primitive mode of development is still retained. Hence, if we regard the most frequent mode of segmentation in *Renilla*—namely, direct division into sixteen spheres—as the normal mode, the occasional division into eight, four, or two may be regarded as cases of reversion to conditions which were once the prevalent modes of development. On the other hand, the single observed case of division into thirty-two spheres shows that while the sixteen-sphere cleavage has been pretty well established, a tendency to further abbreviation still exists. We cannot doubt that if any change of condition should render a further concentration of development advantageous, this tendency or capability would come into play, and a segmentation like that of the Insecta might be produced.

As the various forms of regular cleavage may be explained as the result of variations in the amount of equally distributed deutoplasm (or in the activity of the protoplasm), so we may in part explain the various forms of unequal segmentation as due to variations in the distribution of the deutoplasm. As shown in figs. 55–57 certain spheres may be slower in their development than others, so that their descendants are larger, a fact long since observed by ALLMAN in Hydroid eggs. This is probably caused by the presence of a larger amount of deutoplasm than common, though possibly to the tardy division of the nuclei. In the forms of "partial" segmentation shown in figs. 59–67, the large unsegmented mass must contain a number of fully formed nuclei, since it breaks up almost at once into several spheres. Hence the delay is caused, apparently, by some obstacle in the vitellus, which we may suppose to be an especially great amount of deutoplasm in one half of the egg, as is normally the case in the entodermic pole of an epibolic gastrula. It is possible in this case also to suppose that the delay is due to tardy multiplication of the nuclei, but this explanation seems less probable than the other. In some cases the small spheres are gradually constricted off from the unsegmented part, and the egg may pass into a resting stage, leaving a number of spheres only half formed (see figs. 59, 60, 63, 64). This fact strongly indicates that there is some resistance to be overcome in the vitellus, for there can be little doubt that the half-formed spheres contain fully developed nuclei.

There are a number of other facts which point in the same direction. The first formed cleavage furrows penetrate very slowly towards the centre of the ovum and, in some cases at least, do not reach the centre during the first stage of activity. The segmentation is at first, therefore, of the type which BALFOUR has termed *centrolecithal*, the egg consisting of a peripheral layer of partially-formed cells and a solid central yolk-mass. The egg differs somewhat in structure, however, from a typical centrolecithal ovum; for the central yolk-mass, so far as can be determined, does not contain at this period a greater proportion of deutoplasm than the peripheral parts, though it does so at a later stage. The failure of the cleavage furrows to reach the centre of the egg seems to be due either to the resistance being greater in the central parts, or to the exhaustion of the energy of the protoplasm before the inertia of the entire mass of deutoplasm has been overcome.

It is interesting to compare *Renilla* in this respect with *Clavularia* on the one hand and *Alcyonium* on the other, as described by KOWALEVSKY. In *Clavularia* the resistance of the entire mass of deutoplasm would seem to be less than in *Renilla*, as the egg divides completely and regularly from the first. In *Alcyonium*, on the other hand, the resistance in the central mass is greater than in *Renilla*, and the segmentation does not affect the central portions of the egg for some time. Irregular protoplasmic protuberances separate themselves from the yolk to form segmentation spheres, which after a time arrange themselves in a simple regular ectodermic layer. The central mass remains, for a considerable time, quite unsegmented, but finally breaks up into large rounded entoderm cells. Hence it appears that the cleavages do not reach the centre of the egg until the delamination takes place; and in this case the cause seems pretty clearly to lie in the greater abundance of deutoplasm in the central portion of the egg.

The principle that unequal distribution of deutoplasm produces unequal rates of development in different parts of the egg, will not, however, account for some of the forms of unequal segmentation in *Renilla*. When, for instance, the egg divides into four larger and four smaller spheres, the former do not contain a greater number of nuclei than the latter, since at the following cleavage all are divided alike into two parts, and further, we have seen that the inequality existing at first may be considerably reduced without the occurrence of any visible cleavage. It is improbable that the cause is simply a lack of precision in the action of the vitellus, since the arrangement of the spheres is constant, so far as observed, the larger spheres being at one pole of the egg and the smaller spheres at the other. The resemblance of the egg at this stage to an epibolic gastrula has already been noted, and the idea naturally suggests itself that this resemblance may be due, not to accident, but to actual reversion of the gastrula *form*, though the essential features of the development are entirely different from those of the gastrula. There are a number of facts which indicate the derivation of the delaminate planula from an epibolic gastrula like that of *Euaxes;* and if the planula has had such an origin, it is not improbable that it might occasionally revert to the original unequal form of segmentation.

§ 4. *Changes of external form and further histological differentiation.*

At the close of segmentation the embryo is roughly spherical in form, varying considerably in outline. As development proceeds the body elongates slightly so that a longer axis (antero-posterior) can usually be made out, but the larvæ both of *Renilla* and *Leptogorgia* assume the most irregular and strange forms (figs. 100ᵃ, 100ᵇ, 100ᶜ, 107). Occasionally a larva develops very regularly, preserving a nearly even oval outline until the cilia make their appearance. But in far the greater number large irregular prominences and depressions make their appearance over the whole surface of the embryo, and the form becomes so strangely modified that it is difficult to believe the shrunken and distorted larvæ capable of further development. In fact I unhesitatingly considered them at first as abnormal or dying specimens. No two of them have the same form, and they sometimes appear almost like huge *Amœbæ* with short rounded pseudopodia extended in various directions. Nevertheless the larvæ are perfectly normal, as I repeatedly proved by isolating them in small vessels and following their development. A regular oval form is once more gradually assumed (fig. 101), and most of the larvæ of twenty-four hours show no trace of the strange changes of form through which they have passed. The various prominences and processes are not capable of active movement, and the change of form is exceedingly slow. I am entirely unable to say what the significance of this curious change of form may be, and can hardly find a parallel to it in the development of other animals.

The rate of development varies exceedingly in different individuals, being sometimes twice as rapid as in other cases. In nearly all instances, however, the embryo acquires a dense and uniform covering of cilia when about twenty-four hours old, the body having meanwhile assumed an oval form. The cilia do not at first possess the power of movement, but in a few hours become actively vibratile and propel the larva through the water. As the cilia assume their functional activity the form of the body becomes pyriform, the future oral end being the larger. This form is sometimes marked in the larva of twenty-four hours (fig. 101), but the difference between the oral and aboral extremities is usually less conspicuous than in the specimen figured.

The swimming movements become very active in the thirty-six-hours' larva, and are very characteristic. The larva swims with the aboral end directed forwards, revolving at the same time on the longitudinal axis. The larger (oral) end simply revolves about its centre while the smaller end describes a circle, so that the larva advances by a kind of cork-screw movement. Many of the larvæ swim actively about, but most of them crowd to the surface, where they arrange themselves in rows about the edge with their smaller ends turned upwards and outwards, and, the swimming movements entirely cease. A very similar habit was observed by LACAZE-DUTHIERS in the larvæ of *Astroides*.

By the end of the third day the body becomes elongated (fig. 103), and exceedingly contractile and changeable in form. The larva may be at one moment of a worm-like elongation and at the next instant contract to a short rounded form as in fig. 105. The cilia begin to disappear and the larva swims very sluggishly near the bottom of the aquarium. During the fourth day the cilia entirely disappear and the larvæ sink to the bottom, attaching themselves loosely by means, apparently, of a mucous-like secretion. The larval life is now ended and the tentacles and spicules soon make their appearance (see § 11).

Leptogorgia agrees in the main with *Renilla*, but the development takes place more slowly. The embryo, after passing through the period of distortion, becomes of a regular oval form and acquires a uniform coating of cilia. The aboral end soon becomes slightly smaller and the larva swims with the same peculiar cork-screw movement observed in *Renilla*. The larvæ have the same habit of arranging themselves in rows at the surface of the water. On the fourth day the larvæ are much elongated (fig. 112), and possess the power of active contraction. The larval life is not ended until about the sixth or seventh day, when the cilia disappear, the larva sinks to the bottom and once more assumes a short rounded form (fig. 113), and the eight septa become faintly visible about the eighth day. Some of the larvæ attach themselves firmly by the aboral end, but others remain free as long as they were kept under observation (seven weeks). In one case two larvæ, originally quite distinct, became attached to each other near their oral ends (fig. 114). The union became very complete in a day or two, and no line of division between them could be made out. The larvæ were kept for a fortnight, but underwent very little change, and finally died. I believe their union was due simply to accidental adhesion, and has no significance bearing upon the formation of the colony. KOWALEVSKY observed in *Alcyonium* that numbers of the larvæ fused together in a similar manner, but their subsequent history was not followed. It is very probable that in this case also the union was accidental and was produced by the crowding of the larvæ in small aquaria.

The formation of the septa and tentacles will be described in the following section, and we may now consider the internal histological changes which have been in progress during the stages just described.

At the close of segmentation, the embryo (fig. 97) is a solid planula consisting of a central mass of large rounded cells, enclosed by a layer of cuboidal ectoderm cells. As development proceeds, the cells of both layers continually decrease in size by multiplication, and those of the ectoderm gradually assume a marked columnar form. At the same time, the character of the cell-contents changes somewhat, the deutoplasm spheres disappearing from the ectoderm cells, which accordingly appear less coarsely granular, and remaining only in the central cells, where they continue to be very distinct, until a short time before the appearance of the digestive cavity.

The structure of an embryo of the stage superficially shown by figs. 12 and 13, is well shown in fig. 118. The section figured is from *Leptogorgia*, chosen on account of its good state of preservation; but it agrees in nearly all respects with sections through the corresponding stage of *Renilla*. The outer envelope consists of a single layer of cuboidal cells, in many of which are visible large rounded nuclei. The cells are destitute of membranes. Their contents are granular, but destitute of distinct deutoplasm spheres, and are scarcely stained by the picrocarmine. The peripheral zone of earlier stages is not visible, but in *Renilla* sections of this stage, it appears very clearly, as shown in fig. 119, taken from a somewhat later stage.

The central part of the embryo is occupied with a solid mass of large rounded entoderm cells, or, as they may for the present be called, *central* cells. The latter are enclosed by delicate but distinct membranes, which separate them sharply from each other, and from the surrounding ectoderm. Nuclei are visible in many of them; and some of the larger ones, being in course of division, contain two nuclei. The character of the cell-contents varies somewhat in different parts of the central mass. The more centrally placed cells are closely packed with clear spherules of deutoplasm left unstained by the carmine, between which is a kind of network of finely granular, deeply stained matter. The nuclei appear as clear vesicles, surrounded by deeply stained, finely granular areas. Passing towards the outer portions of the central mass, the deutoplasm spheres become less numerous, disappearing almost entirely in the outermost cells which adjoin the ectoderm.

It is important to notice this early differentiation in the distribution of the deutoplasm; for it indicates either that the deutoplasm is more abundant here even in early stages, when no difference between the central and peripheral parts of the egg is apparent to the eye, or that the protoplasm of the outer portions is more active, and hence assimilates more rapidly the deutoplasm. Either alternative lends support to the view suggested at p. 744, to account for the failure of the earlier cleavage furrows to reach the centre of the egg.

A comparison of figs. 118 and 97 shows that the central mass in the later stage is somewhat greater than in the earlier; and an examination of a number of sections indicates that this difference is a constant one. Hence it seems probable that more than one delamination cleavage may take place, that the central mass may from time to time receive accessions from the outer layer through the occurrence of horizontal cleavages. I have not been able to demonstrate this, though some of my sections give indications of such a process. In some cases the ectoderm cells appear elongated, and as if about to divide in the horizontal plane. It is certain, as will subsequently appear, that such cleavages occur in the ectoderm until a late period, though in later stages, when the supporting lamella is formed, the cells thus produced remain, of course, ectodermic. There seems to be no reason why such cleavages occurring at an early stage should not produce entoderm cells, and such, I am inclined to think, is actually the case.

After the stage shown in fig. 118, however, the cleavages take place for a considerable period mainly in vertical planes, so that the columnar form of the ectoderm cells becomes more and more marked.

The structure of the embryo may be far less regular than is indicated by fig. 118, since the cells often multiply more rapidly over one half of the embryo, and the division of the central cells is often irregular.

Sections through the *Renilla* embryo of about four and a half hours are represented in figs. 119 and 120. The embryo has the same general characters as in the last stage figured, but the cells have largely increased in number. The ectoderm cells have a definitely columnar form, and consist of a granular substance which is not, apparently, enclosed in cell membranes. They are separated by narrow, clear spaces which contain, apparently, a small quantity of intercellular substance. The central cells, on the other hand, are surrounded by definite membranes, which appear in the sections as narrow, dark lines.

There is still no indication of a definite membrane separating the ectoderm from the central mass. The cells of the two layers are to some extent dovetailed together, and have nearly the same structure. Here and there in the ectoderm are rounded or pyriform cells which appear to be in course of division. The clear peripheral zone still appears distinctly at the outer ends of the ectoderm cells. In some specimens it bears a fringe of fine filaments which appear like cilia, but are in reality the remnants of the spermatozoa with which the embryo remains covered for a considerable period.

In the embryo of eight hours (figs. 122–124) the ectoderm layer is sharply differentiated from the central mass, but the latter has undergone very slight change except in the further division of its cells. The ectoderm cells have now a high columnar form, though here and there rounded cells may be observed (fig. 122). At their inner ends, where they are usually somewhat expanded, they abut against the cells of the central mass, and in many parts of the sections are separated from the latter by an irregular, scarcely defined membrane (this is represented as too distinct in the figures). In some sections the membrane does not appear. This membrane appears to be the first rudiment of the supporting lamella ("Stützlamella") which is so characteristic a structure among the polyps and hydroids, but the main body of the lamella is formed somewhat later, as described in the next section. The ectoderm cells now stain very differently from those of the central mass, and the peripheral zone has disappeared. The substance of the cells appears scarcely coloured, while the nuclei are deeply stained. The central cells, on the other hand, stain deeply, so as to be very sharply differentiated from the ectoderm in colour as well as in form. The deutoplasm spheres have the same distribution as in earlier stages, being very abundant and clearly defined in the more centrally placed cells (fig. 124) and becoming indistinct and scanty, or quite disappearing in the outer cells. There is still not the least trace of a digestive cavity.

I am unable to say what the significance of the peripheral zone may be. A very similar zone is described by HOFFMANN in the ectoderm cells of *Tetrastemma* at an early stage and by RABL in the ectoderm of *Unio*. It is possibly concerned in the formation of the cilia, but this seems improbable, since it disappears in *Renilla* long before the cilia are formed.

In this stage the sections of the embryo sometimes appear exactly as if taken from an epibolic gastrula, for the ectoderm cells may be very different both in size and form on opposite sides of the embryo. This appearance is however entirely deceptive, and is produced simply by the tardy multiplication of the cells over one half of the embryo.

§ 5. *Formation of the entoderm and appearance of the digestive cavity.*

The embryo has thus far remained quite solid with no trace of a digestive cavity. For some hours longer this condition continues, the only change consisting in the multiplication of the cells of both layers. About the twentieth hour, however, or at the time when the cilia make their first appearance, peculiar changes become evident in the central cells which are the forerunner of the formation of the proper entoderm and the stomach cavity. The deutoplasm spheres disappear completely from the central cells, which then have a coarsely and irregularly granular appearance with very distinct membranes and deeply stained nuclei. The central mass is still solid, however, and the cells are all of the same irregularly rounded form. In a few hours a very perceptible difference can be seen between the outer and the inner cells of the central mass. Those which lie just beneath the ectoderm (figs. 125 and 126, *en.*) become much clearer, their substance stains very little, and many of them assume a slightly columnar form. Their nuclei are very distinct, of a slightly oval form, and very deeply stained. The cells are in some parts of the larva arranged in a single layer, but in other parts seem to be placed two or more deep.   It is difficult in this, as in subsequent stages, to say whether this appearance of several layers in the entoderm may not be due to the sections being always more or less oblique in different parts of the section ; but I believe, after examination, that they do form several layers in some parts of the embryo at this stage.   This layer of clear cells is the permanent or true entoderm.

The central cells, on the other hand, remain rounded and very granular, and stain more deeply than the entoderm cells.   They become ultimately disorganised and are absorbed as food by the true entoderm cells ; hence they may hereafter conveniently be termed the *yolk-cells*.

The yolk-cells form at first a solid mass which is directly continuous with the entoderm cells surrounding it.   Soon, however (fig. 125), the yolk-cells become more loosely connected, and considerable cavities appear in the central mass in which the yolk-cells often lie quite disconnected from the other cells or united in groups of two or more cells.   It is difficult to gain a clear idea of the changes which bring about this condition.   Apparently the entire larva increases somewhat in size while the membranes of the yolk-cells become partially disorganised.   In parts of the yolk-mass the cell-contents with their nuclei seem actually to drop out of the cell-membranes, which remain as a delicate network (fig. 126) in which the form of the cells is still perfectly preserved.   Possibly this occurs only as a result of rough handling after the sections are made.   Still I believe it may be in part a normal occurrence and that some at least of the free naked cells in the yolk-cavities may have been thus liberated.   Others of the free cells have at first delicate cell-membranes, but these afterwards disappear.

The yolk-cells are rounded, but vary greatly in form and size.   Most of them are still distinctly nucleated, but the nuclei are less sharply defined and have less regular outlines than those of the entoderm cells.   The cell-substance contains no deutoplasm spheres, and consists of a granular substance which stains irregularly and in some places not at all.   Besides the yolk-cells there is a considerable quantity of granular substance in the form of small balls or masses lying in the yolk-cavities, and here and there may be seen a deeply stained free nucleus surrounded by a small quantity of granular matter.   It is probable that the granular matter is derived from the breaking down of the yolk-cells, but it is difficult to say how far these appearances are the result of normal phenomena of disintegration, and how far due simply to mechanical injuries produced by manipulation.   The general features of a section of this stage (twenty-two and a half hours) are well shown in fig. 125.

Still later the yolk-mass becomes completely disorganised, breaking up into a kind of *débris* in which several distinct elements can be recognised (fig. 127).   There are : firstly, rounded cells with distinct nuclei and membranes, which are simply free yolk-cells ; second, similar but usually smaller cells which have no membrane ; third, free nuclei which are usually associated with a small quantity of granular matter ; fourth, small rounded granular bodies, about one-fourth the size of the yolk-cells and destitute of nuclei ; and fifth, still smaller granules, apparently produced by the disintegration of the preceding.

The entoderm (*en.*) has now a very different appearance from that of the last stage. The cells are columnar, with very distinct oval nuclei, which are always situated in the outer half of the cells ; but the cell-contents are dark and opaque, being densely packed with granules. The cell-outlines are thus more or less obscured, and though always distinct towards the outer part of the cell may be quite invisible towards the base. The granulation is of quite different appearance in the inner and outer parts of the cells. In the basal (*i.e.*, outer) part the granules are fine and closely packed, and are left nearly or quite unstained, while in the inner ends of the cells the granulation is coarse and irregular, and stains more readily. This difference is so constant that in most specimens the basal granulation forms a pretty distinct narrow zone extending around the entire entoderm. The cells are in some parts of the sections only one layer deep, but in other parts the entoderm consists of several layers and varies greatly in thickness.

The general features of a twenty-nine-hours' larva are shown in fig. 128, and a portion of the body-wall, more highly magnified, in fig. 129. The body is now distinctly elongated and the oral end can be distinguished by its greater size. The entoderm is composed of high columnar cells, and is everywhere much thicker than the ectoderm. The gastric cavity is clearly defined and the yolk-mass is greatly reduced in bulk. Under a high power (fig. 129) the yolk-cells are found to have nearly disappeared, though here and there one may still be recognised. The yolk is almost entirely composed of the naked granular spheroidal bodies described in the last stage. They vary a good deal in size, but are on the average rather larger than the nuclei of the entoderm cells. They appear to have had their origin in the breaking up of the yolk-cells, though some of them are perhaps small yolk-cells which have lost their nuclei.

The entoderm cells (*en.*) are much elongated and present some interesting characters. Towards their bases they are filled as before with fine granules, which stain very slightly, and are arranged in a distinct zone encircling the entire larva. Their inner portions (apical) present a confused coarsely granular appearance, entirely unlike that of the basal granulation. The cells seem to contain rounded granular masses, which have the same appearance as the smaller spheroidal bodies of the yolk, which lie outside the cells in the stomach cavity. As in the last stage, the granules are so abundant that it is difficult to make out the outlines of the cells, which only appear clear and well defined at their inner ends.

The yolk gradually disappears as development progresses and the larva rapidly increases in size. Much variation exists in the length of time required for absorption, but it is always complete, so far as I have observed, by the forty-eighth hour, and the gastric cavity is left empty, or sometimes containing a small quantity of a delicate *débris*, which appears to be the remains of the membranes of the yolk-cells. After the yolk is completely absorbed the contents of the entoderm cells again change their character, as shown in fig. 130 (fifty-two hours). They become once more clear, and the basal granulation nearly disappears. The cells still contain a considerable quantity of granules, but the contrast with the preceding stages is marked. The cell-outlines consequently become much more distinct. The nuclei are deeply stained, very conspicuous, and are situated always in the inner parts of the cells.

Conclusions.

Although I have made many sections of larvæ prepared by various methods while yolk-absorption was in progress, I have failed to obtain decisive evidence as to the precise *modus operandi* by which the yolk-cells or their remains are absorbed by the entoderm cells. This failure is due to the excessive minuteness and delicacy of the tissues which renders it extremely difficult to make satisfactory preparations of them. But a careful study of the sections inclines me to the belief that the smaller particles of the yolk-*débris* are engulphed bodily by the entoderm cells Amœba-fashion, the process of digestion being completed within the body of the cell : that, in other words, the young *Renilla* is nourished by a form of intra-cellular digestion. As we have seen, the cells are at first clear and nearly destitute of granules. They become granular, however, and increase in size as soon as the disintegration of the yolk-cells begins, and their granular appearance continues until the absorption of the yolk is completed, when they become again clearer. The large, coarse granules in their inner ends (*i.e.*, those turned towards the yolk-mass) have the same appearance as the small yolk-granules lying just outside the cells, and the entoderm often contain rounded granular masses which are very similar, though with less distinct outlines, to the yolk-spheroids of the digestive cavity. The spheroids may often be observed to lie directly upon the entoderm cells, and the inner ends of the latter are sometimes produced into small amœboid processes reaching out into the digestive cavity, though this is rare.

These appearances suggest, though they do not prove, that the yolk-granules and spheroids pass bodily into the cells. I have never seen them in the act of passing into the cells, but the technical difficulties are great, and the other considerations seem of sufficient weight to warrant the provisional acceptance of the view advanced above.

This conclusion, if well-founded, is of interest in connexion with recent discoveries in regard to intra-cellular digestion in Cœlenterata and Turbellaria. The occurrence of such a form of digestion in the sponges has long been a familiar fact, and the more recent researches of METSCHNIKOFF, CLAUS, GEGENBAUR, PARKER and RAY LANKESTER have shown that an essentially similar mode of digestion occurs in the adults of many Cœlenterata belonging to the higher groups, namely : in *Hydra*, Hydroid polyps, Hydromedusæ, Acalephs, Actiniæ, Ctenophora and Siphonophora. METSCHNIKOFF showed in 1878 that the same remarkable process takes place in a number of fresh water Turbellaria, and he has ascribed to it an important phylogenetic significance. He points out the fact that intra-cellular or amœboid digestion is confined, so far as known, to the most primitive groups of the Metazoa and in the Cœlenterates seems to be the normal and most frequent if not the only process. The digestive functions of an entoderm cell in these cases are identical with those of a unicellular Protozoa, and METSCHNIKOFF is inclined to consider the former as an actual survival of the latter—a physiological character which was originally present in all Metazoa then existing, and has only been lost in higher forms. LANKESTER even suggests that the absorption of unsaponified fats in the highest Metazoa may possibly be a last relic of the primitive mode of digestion.

None of the writers on this subject have pointed out the identity of the process with that of the absorption of the yolk in *Astacus*, described by REICHENBACH in 1877 (Zeitschrift für Wiss. Zool., Bd. xxix., 1877). In this case the amœba-like action of the entoderm cells was observed with the greatest clearness. The cells put forth large pseudopodia, and actively engulph the yolk-granules which were observed in every stage of the passage from the yolk-mass into the cell-bodies. The ingestion takes place, it is true, at the basal instead of the apical end of the cells, since the yolk lies outside the archenteron ; but this circumstance does not tell against the identity of the process with that of adult Cœlenterata and Turbellaria and of the larval *Renilla*. WOLFSON has observed a similar process in the yolk-absorption of *Lymnæus*, and in this case the nutriment, as in *Renilla*, is contained within the archenteron (see Bulletin de l'Académie Impériale des Sciences de Saint-Pétersbourg, tom. xxvi., pp. 79–99, 1880. Lu le 9 Octobre, 1879).

It is interesting to find the embryonic entoderm cells exhibiting this primitive mode of digestion, though it is clearly to be regarded simply as an adaptation connected with the presence of a large amount of food-yolk. Still the idea is suggested that the amœba-like ingestion of food in the larva may perhaps be due to a kind of reversion, the reappearance in the larva of a feature which, in the case of *Astacus* and *Lymnæus* at least, has become quite dormant in the adult. Whether it exists in the adult *Renilla* I have been unable to determine, but it cannot be observed in the young transparent colonies (see p. 786).

Whatever be the mode of absorption, the granular basal zone, so often referred to, appears to be a reserve store of food-material—either the actual remains of the ingested food-granules, or a new store of granules laid up for future use by the protoplasm after being richly fed. It would seem that the cell packs away its reserve supply of food in its basal part, leaving the apical or inner end free to continue the active work of feeding ; so that there is in a sense a physiological division of labour within the cell. It is noteworthy that the entoderm nucleus is invariably situated in the inner part of the cell which contains the coarser granules. This position of the entoderm nuclei appears to be not uncommon in embryos where the gastric cavity is filled with food material (compare *Lumbricus*, t. KLEINENBERG, and *Planorbis*, t. RABL) ; and RABL has suggested in the case of *Planorbis* that they play a part in the absorptive activity of the cells. I have not been able to discover any such function in the nuclei.

§ 6. *Comparison with other forms.*

Upon comparing the formation of the digestive cavity in *Renilla* with that of other Anthozoa, we find, in some cases, a close agreement, but in other cases the phenomena are entirely different. All of the Alcyonarian forms, so far as known, excepting *Monoxenia*, agree in their general features with *Renilla*, developing as solid delaminate planulas, in which the gastric cavity is hollowed out by the disintegration and absorption of a central mass of yolk-cells, and the latter are at first indistinguishable from the true or permanent entoderm cells. *Gorgonia*, according to KOWALEVSKY, is an exception to the rule ; for the embryo contains a central cavity surrounded by a layer of ciliated rounded cells, which are in turn enclosed in a layer of columnar true entoderm cells. The ciliated cells are believed by KOWALEVSKY to be absorbed, and are considered as homologous with the yolk-cells of other forms. It is noteworthy that *Leptogorgia*, though far more nearly allied to *Gorgonia* than to *Renilla*, agrees entirely in development with the latter, and does not have a permanent segmentation cavity.

Among the Zoantharia, the greater number of forms agree with the Alcyonaria in developing as solid delaminate planulæ in which the gastric cavity is formed by the absorption of a central yolk-mass. A few forms, on the other hand, viz.: *Cerianthus* (KOWALEVSKY, JOURDAN), *Actinia equina* L. (JOURDAN), and perhaps an allied *Actinia*, and probably *Caryophyllium* (KOWALEVSKY), develop as invaginate gastrulæ. BALFOUR states, on the authority of KLEINENBERG, that in some of the apparently delaminate types the segmentation is unequal, which "probably indicates an epibolic gastrula." While the occurrence of epibolic gastrulæ among these forms is by no means improbable, it cannot be accepted on this evidence alone ; for the segmentation of *Renilla* shows that such an inference may be entirely false.

It is a curious fact that in two at least of the invaginate forms, viz. : *Actina equina* (JOURDAN), and *Cerianthus* (KOWALEVSKY), a yolk-mass is formed in the gastric cavity some time after the invagination has occurred, though no traces of it exist in earlier stages. Thus, of the former species JOURDAN states : " L'espace entre les cloisons est toujours occupé par une masse probablement vitelline, et qu'on croirait exsudée des tissus de la larve ; cette masse nutritive est formée par de grosses vésicules semblables à des cellules adipeuses et par des noyaux fortement colorés par les réactifs."[*] KOWALEVSKY regards the yolk-mass of *Cerianthus* as a secretion of the deeper layers of the entoderm, and considers its elements as fat globules. In both cases the yolk-mass is eventually resorbed. If the origin of the yolk-mass is correctly described by these eminent observers, it is clearly not homologous with that of the Alcyonarian forms.

[*] Ann. d. Sci. Nat., 6me série, tome x., p. 129.

The phenomena of the yolk-absorption have not been carefully studied, and it is therefore impossible to draw any general conclusions in regard to the significance of the processes described for *Renilla.* An examination of JOURDAN's descriptions and figures of the larvæ of *Balanophyllia regia* (GOSSE) leaves in my mind little doubt that in this case also the yolk is ingested *Amœba*-fashion by the entoderm cells, though JOURDAN himself puts an entirely different interpretation on his own observations, as may be seen from the following extracts. He says of the entoderm cells at an early stage (*l.c.*, p. 134): " Elles sont très volumineuses, allongées, contiennent des nucléoles fortement colorés par les réactifs *et de grandes vésicules hyalines*. Au centre de la masse vitelline constituant l'endoderme, ces cellules disparaissent, les vésicules hyalines persistent seules" (the italics are my own). In later stages, when six or more septa have appeared : "Sur les coupes transversales, les grandes cellules situées au bord externe de l'entoderme des larves vermiformes ont disparu ; les vésicules hyalines persistent et forment la totalité de la masse entodermique." In later stages, however, when the yolk is absorbed, as shown by his figure of the adult entoderm (*l.c.*, fig. 110, plate 15), the cells come into view again, having the same form as before, but rarely containing the "vésicules hyalines."

It appears in the highest degree improbable that the entoderm cells should completely disappear to be subsequently re-developed in precisely the same form. A far more credible conclusion is that the yolk-vesicles are taken bodily into the cells in such numbers as finally to obscure the cell-outlines entirely. The entoderm then seems to have disappeared and only makes its re-appearance when the yolk-vesicles have been assimilated by the protoplasm of the cells. This conclusion is strengthened by the fact that in JOURDAN's figure of the larva of *Actinia equina* (*l.c.*, fig. 119, plate 16) the entoderm cells are figured, before the absorption of the yolk has begun, as clear, well defined, and destitute of yolk-vesicles, while the gastric cavity is completely filled with "vésicules hyalines" precisely like those of *Balanophyllia.* This condition, according to my view, precedes one like the earlier stage of *Balanophyllia* in which absorption has recently begun and in which the entoderm cells resemble those of *Astacus*, as figured by REICHENBACH.[*]

In all known Alcyonarians the central mass, though at first unsegmented, does sooner or later divide into cells, although many of these perform no active function, become disorganised, and serve only as food for other cells. This indicates that the yolk-cells are the descendants of cells which were once of structural significance ; for otherwise their formation and subsequent disintegration would seem to be a sheer waste of energy. They are identical in origin and structure with the permanent entoderm cells, and are undoubtedly homologous with the latter. Hence we may infer that the yolk-cells were originally functional entoderm cells in which deutoplasm accumulated to such an extent that they became devoted solely to the storing of food for the embryo. The remaining entoderm cells retained their functional

[*] Zeitschr. für Wiss. Zool., Bd. xxix., 1877.

activity as digestive cells, and by an early development of this function in the embryo became capable of digesting the yolk-cells precisely as if the latter were foreign food-matters introduced through the mouth. How such a two-fold specialisation of the entoderm cells was possible is shown in the embryo of *Gorgonia*; for in this case the yolk-cells still persist in an apparently functional state, being ciliated and surrounding a central cavity. Only a step before this is the planula of *Gorgonia* or *Liriope* (METSCHNIKOFF and FOL) in which the central cavity exists from the first and all the delaminated entoderm cells persist as such.

If we push this speculation further and inquire after the causes which originally determined that some of the primitive entoderm cells should persist as such while others became yolk-cells, we encounter a very broad question, which it would be hardly profitable to enter upon here, since it belongs too exclusively at present to the region of pure speculation. The question is of the same nature, for instance, as that concerning the influence which determines the survival of a particular cell of the germinal epithelium of the ovary, as an ovum, while its neighbours are absorbed, or remain as simple epithelial cells.[*] We can only say that the differentiation probably stood in some relation with the relative position of the cells; for only the peripheral cells persist as entoderm cells. This suggests that the divergence may have depended upon, or is at least now directly determined by, differences in the supply of oxygen afforded to the cells—in other words is due to respiratory differences. The peripheral cells being nearer to the exterior, must command a more plentiful supply of oxygen, and in this respect have a decided advantage over the inner cells. This may be enough to determine the survival of the former and the disintegration of the latter.

According to a theory of WEISSMANN's, the cells of the ovary (in *Leptodora*) attain a certain "maximal development," which is a critical point in the life of a cell. If it receive an additional impulse, though a very slight one, it continues to develop into an ovum at the expense of its less fortunate neighbours. If, on the other hand, it does not receive this impulse, the cell loses its power of development and is absorbed by the developing ova. The determining impulse is believed by WEISSMANN to be a slight advantage of nutrition which is potent because acting at a critical moment. Such a theory of "maximal development" would seem to apply well in the present case, but the impulse to development does not seem to be in any way connected with general nutrition but only with the supply of oxygen. The theory, though resting perhaps on a rather slender basis, has the merit of showing how a very slight difference in the supply of oxygen might determine the survival or the degeneration of the cells.

* See on this point WEISSMANN, "Ueber die Bildung von Wintereiern bei *Leptodora hyalina*," Zeitz. f. Wiss. Zool., Bd. xxvii., 1876, who has given an elaborate discussion of the question in the case of the ova of the Cladocera.

§ 7. *Changes in the ectoderm and formation of the supporting lamella.*

In the larva of eight hours, as already described, there is a delicate sinuous membrane lying between the ectoderm and entoderm, upon which the cells of the former are planted as upon a basement membrane. This is perhaps the first beginning of the characteristic supporting lamella, but it is far less well defined and less conspicuous than in later stages, and the great bulk of the lamella is formed somewhat later by a peculiar transformation of the inner ends of the ectoderm cells. It is difficult to determine the origin of this preliminary membrane, but appearances indicate that it is secreted by the expanded bases of the ectoderm cells. The membrane varies much in appearance and is sometimes quite invisible even in much later stages. It is often apparent in one part of a section and quite invisible in other parts, while the true lamella, once formed, is remarkably constant and distinct.

The ectoderm cells of this stage have a high columnar form, which, though ultimately lost, is retained throughout the succeeding stages until a late period. At intervals, however, the cells rapidly proliferate (fig. 131, twenty-eight hours), and the columnar form may at these times be temporarily lost, the cells assuming various rounded forms and becoming in many cases entirely separated from the underlying entoderm cells. The division of the cells takes place both in horizontal and vertical planes, so that the ectoderm gradually becomes several layers deep. At the close of a period of proliferation most of the cells resume the high columnar form, some of them extending through the entire thickness of the ectoderm, others extending inwards from the surface and terminating by attenuated extremities without reaching the entoderm. Others, again, are placed with their broader end—which contains the nucleus—lying near the bottom of the ectoderm, and others still are of a fusiform shape with the thickest part containing the nucleus, near the middle of the ectoderm. The structure of the ectoderm at this stage is very like that of *Heliopora* (MOSELEY, Phil. Trans., Vol. 166, 1876).

Besides the columnar cells there are others of a rounded form with centrally placed nuclei, which lie in the deeper parts of the ectoderm or in the narrow clear space which often separates the layers; they often lie directly on the outer ends of the entoderm cells. These never return to the columnar form and persist throughout the entire development. They give rise to elements of the so-called mesoderm, some of them becoming the matrices for the development of the spicules, and others remaining as peculiar rounded cells which are possibly nerve-cells.

In the larva of about twenty-two hours (figs. 125, 132), the basal ends of the columnar ectoderm cells undergo a peculiar change of form and structure. They separate completely from the entoderm, become smoothly rounded, the character of the granulation changes, and they stain less readily than before. At the same time a large quantity of a finely granular substance makes its appearance in the space between the ectoderm and entoderm (figs. 125, 133). This space is sometimes very

wide on account of the shrinkage of the central mass, but even in this case is sometimes nearly filled with the granular matter. The appearance of the granular mass
varies greatly in different specimens and in different parts of the same section. It may
be very abundant and of a loose flocculent character in one part, while elsewhere it
gradually disappears and is replaced by a definite membrane lying between the
ectoderm and entoderm, which is unmistakably the supporting lamella. In favourable
specimens the granular mass may be traced around the section, becoming more and
more closely compacted until it passes directly into the supporting lamella.

These facts leave no doubt that the supporting lamella is derived from the
granular mass, which becomes compacted together to form a definite membrane. The
granular mass probably never has naturally any considerable thickness, being compacted into the membrane as soon as it is formed. The loose flocculent character is
probably produced by the action of the reagents which causes the material of the
supporting lamella to swell up, while the central mass at the same time shrinks away
from the ectoderm, forming the cavity in which the granular mass lies.

In fig. 133, which will illustrate the appearance of a section at this period, there
are parts of the section where neither granules nor lamella appear, other parts where
the outer ends of the entoderm cells are covered only by their own cell-membranes
outside of which is a small quantity of granular matter; while in other portions a
pretty distinct lamella is formed with abundant granular matter outside of it. The
entoderm cells show no change at any time during the formation of the lamella.
This indicates that the ectoderm alone is concerned in the production of the granular
matter which forms the lamella, and this conclusion is confirmed by a study of the
ectoderm cells. The inner ends of the cells are rounded and swollen and
often terminate in knob-like swellings (fig. 132, b.), attached to the bodies of the
cells by narrow necks. These swollen inner ends then separate from the bodies of
the cells and lie in the deeper parts of the ectoderm or in the space between the
two layers. In some specimens, of which fig. 132 is a good example, the lower
part of the ectoderm is closely packed with these rounded bodies, of which some are
still attached to the cells, but most are free. The substance of which these balls are
composed is quite like the granular substance, and the balls may be seen in various
stages of disintegration.

Hence we may conclude that the material of the supporting lamella is derived from
the disintegrated granular balls which have separated from the ectoderm cells. It is
possible that the swollen inner ends do not normally separate bodily from the ectoderm
cells and that this is accidentally done in making the sections. This is hardly probable,
however, since the outlines of the granular masses are usually regular, and they are
found free in large numbers. The granular bodies appear in some cases to discharge their
contents without breaking down and losing their form. I conclude this from the
occasional presence of clear, rounded bodies in the granular mass of the same form and
size as the granular bodies. These clear bodies (several of which are shown in fig. 133)

appear to be surrounded by delicate membranes and become in some cases incorporated into the substance of the supporting lamella. They are not to be confounded with the rounded nucleated cells which are sometimes also found in the granular mass and may likewise become incorporated into the lamella. Besides the latter, cellular elements derived from the entoderm may in some cases enter into the composition of the lamella. Now and then an entoderm cell (see figs. 125 and 132) may flatten down, become incapable of development and become incorporated with the mass of the lamella.

After the secretion of the granular matter is completed the cells re-assume their high columnar form with their inner ends often resting upon the lamella as on a basement membrane (figs. 127–130). The latter appears as a very distinct, narrow, structureless membrane sharply separated from the ectoderm and entoderm. Outside of it is usually a narrow, clear space, but the granular matter has entirely disappeared. This condition of the ectoderm is maintained until the sixtieth or seventieth hour, when the ectoderm totally changes its character. The lamella remains unchanged up to the latest stage of the colony observed, without increasing in thickness or undergoing visible change of structure.

Review.

The material of the lamella is derived from the cells of the ectoderm by a peculiar form of cuticular secretion, which consists in the separation of rounded granular masses from the inner ends of the cells. The formation of these bodies is a process entirely different from cell-division since the nuclei do not divide, and they remain quite unchanged during the process. The granular bodies in most cases disintegrate, but sometimes appear to discharge their contents as in ordinary secretion. Possibly the ectoderm cells may also in some cases discharge the contents of their swollen basal ends without the separation of a part of the cell, but this must, I believe, be exceptional. The mode of secretion described is a very anomalous one, and appears to stand midway between the disintegration and discharge of an entire cell during secretion, as in the formation of "goblet-cells" in mucous glands, and the more usual forms of secretion in which the product exudes from the cell without the destruction of the latter.

The formation of the supporting lamella in other forms has not been worked out with sufficient care to afford any basis for comparison. KOWALEVSKY concluded that the lamella in *Actinia* is secreted by the entoderm, since it penetrates into the septa, which are entirely entodermic. This is, however, an unwarrantable conclusion ; for, as will be shown later, the lamella of the radial septa has an entirely different origin from that of the peduncular septum, and both differ in origin from that of the body-wall. It is evident that the supporting lamella, though probably containing cellular elements derived both from the ectoderm and entoderm, is not in any sense a special mesodermic layer, but has only the significance of a structureless cuticular membrane separating and supporting the two fundamental layers of the body.

II.

DEVELOPMENT OF ORGANS AND TISSUES.

The larva now consists of a layer of ectoderm and entoderm separated by the supporting lamella and enclosing the gastric cavity. The latter has as yet no communication with the exterior and shows no trace of division into the eight radiating chambers characteristic of all Alcyonarian polyps. Within a few hours— usually between the fortieth and fiftieth—the œsophagus is formed, though it is not perforated until a far later period, and the gastric cavity is divided into chambers through the appearance of radiating septa. These structures develop simultaneously, but it will be convenient to follow their formation separately, and the same plan will be followed in describing the development of other organs.

§ 8. *Formation of the œsophagus and mouth.*

The œsophagus usually makes its appearance in the larva of about forty hours as a solid invagination of ectoderm at the larger end of the body (fig. 134). The high columnar ectoderm cells at this point change their form entirely and rapidly multiply, and are pushed into the body of the larva as a solid plug (fig. 134, *st.*). The invaginated cells are very small, rounded, possess distinct but very small nuclei, and are so closely packed together that their outlines can scarcely be distinguished except in very thin sections. They differ widely from the entoderm cells, being far smaller, staining more deeply and of a different tint, and their nuclei are much smaller. In some cases the œsophagus contains from the first a very small cavity extending inwards from the exterior, but it is usually quite solid. As the plug of ectoderm is pushed in, it carries before it the supporting lamella and the entoderm, the cells of the latter multiplying at the same time. These entodermic cells assume a high columnar form, with their long axes directed towards the œsophagus (fig. 134).

The ectodermic plug grows rapidly backwards and assumes a somewhat pyriform shape from the expansion of its lower extremity (fig. 136), and the entoderm, which everywhere covers it, often becomes much thickened, especially at its lower end. A narrow cavity (fig. 135) then appears in its centre, communicating at the anterior extremity with the exterior, but still ending blindly below. The cavity appears to be formed by the giving way of the central cells, aided to some extent, perhaps, by absorption. In this stage the cells towards the outer opening sometimes have an obscurely columnar form, but towards the inner end of the invagination are small and rounded as before. The cavity at its very first appearance, as shown in transverse sections, is greatly elongated in a particular direction, which is always the same in relation to the septa and is shown by the later development to coincide with the dorso-ventral axis.

The œsophagus remains in this condition for a considerable period (twenty to twenty-five hours), during which the only change consists in the clear definition of the cavity and the expansion of its lower end (fig 136). In most cases the lower angles of the cavity are prolonged downwards so that the cavity has a distinct Y-shape; this form is sometimes much more pronounced than in the figure. The cavity then breaks through, thus placing the gastric cavity for the first time in communication with the exterior.

I have made many sections, longitudinal and transverse, through the œsophagus at this period, a study of which leaves little doubt that great variation exists in the formation of the mouth, as in so many other features of the development. The most common mode is illustrated by figs. 137–140. The wall of the œsophagus thins away by absorption at one of the lower angles of the Y (fig. 131) and finally breaks away at this point (fig. 139). At the opposite side the mass of tissue forming the bottom of the œsophagus still remains attached to the lateral wall of the œsophagus and to the edges of the septa which have meanwhile been formed. As the septa grow backwards this mass of tissue (which for the sake of convenience I shall call the *œsophageal plug*) is carried down with them, being attached to the edges of one or more of them (fig. 140), sometimes by a narrow neck. The mass of tissue is then gradually absorbed and the œsophagus is left in free communication with the gastric cavity. In several of my specimens, at this stage, a large mass of tissue may be observed lying in the gastric cavity below the œsophagus. This is quite similar in appearance to the œsophageal plug, and is, I believe, identical with it. Hence it would appear that in some cases absorption takes place all around the œsophageal plug, which finally drops out bodily into the gastric cavity and is there absorbed as if it were food or yolk-material. In a number of specimens, one of which is shown in fig. 141, a still different mode was observed. Absorption here begins near the middle of the bottom of the œsophagus between the two arms of the Y-shaped cavity and the opening at length breaks through at this point, leaving the remains of the œsophageal plug attached to the lips of the œsophagus where they are absorbed.

During these changes the layer of ectoderm forming the bottom of the œsophageal cavity becomes indistinct, and in most cases the supporting lamella which separates it from the underlying mass of entoderm disappears. The cells of both layers in the plug change their character and are no longer differentiated by the staining fluid, so that the œsophageal plug appears to be composed of uniform confused granular cells. In one of my specimens (fig. 159) the greater part of the œsophageal plug seems to have been absorbed, leaving the supporting lamella stretching across the œsophageal cavity. Below this is a mass of delicate *débris*, which is apparently the last remains of the œsophageal plug.

Review.

The earlier view, according to which the œsophagus is to be regarded as a stomach, opening below into the body cavity, is now entirely abandoned. In view of its embryological history, the œsophagus is apparently a true stomodæum, comparable to that of the higher Metazoa. The general occurrence of this structure—which, so far as the evidence at command shows, is homologous throughout all the groups in which it is found—is a very striking fact which probably has an important phylogenetic significance. Its universal occurrence among the Anthozoa and complete absence from the Hydrozoa is a strong argument in favour of the more primitive nature of the latter group. From the fact that the Anthozoa are the most primitive group in which the stomodæum appears, it might be concluded that this group represents the stock from which the higher Metazoa have descended. It seems, however, much more probable that the line of descent has been through some primitive Turbellarian form which, in common with the polyps, derived the stomodæum from a still earlier group. What this origin of the stomodæum was is still an unsolved problem. The hypothesis that the stomodæum is to be regarded as the introverted manubrium of a Hydrozoan, though a plausible one, has no embryological facts in its favour, and can hardly be accepted without additional evidence.

§ 9. *Development of the septa.*

The septa make their appearance at about the same time with the stomodæum, and are well developed within a few hours. As we shall see below, the eight radial septa of the anterior part of the body, which are characteristic of all Alcyonaria, differ entirely in structure and mode of origin from the peduncular septum, a structure which is found in the Pennatulacea alone. Hence it will be convenient to describe separately the development of the two forms of septa.

a. Formation of the radial septa.

Although the peduncular septum makes its appearance some time before the radial septa, it is preferable to describe the development of the latter first. They make their appearance simultaneously at the oral extremity of the larva at the time when the stomodæal invagination takes place, and gradually extend thence backwards about to the middle of the body. Although I have made many sections through the septa at the time of their first appearance, and have given special attention to the matter, I have not been able to discover any difference in the time of their appearance. In later stages, as described further on, they are of different lengths, and the differences are perfectly constant. This is, however, the only indication of a regular succession in the development of the septa, and in the earlier stages no difference can be observed.

The septa appear upon longitudinal section (fig. 136, fifty-two hours) as thick plates of entoderm cells (*s.s.*) extending downwards from the oral end and ending by free edges below. Inwardly they are continuous with the entoderm covering the stomodæum; outwardly they join the entoderm of the body-wall. In transverse section (fig. 142) they are seen to radiate at nearly equal intervals from the stomodæum. The centre of each is occupied by a delicate supporting lamella, continuous outwardly with that of the body-wall, and inwardly with that which separates the ectodermic and entodermic layers of the œsophagus. The entoderm cells are arranged upon both sides of the lamella in a thick irregular layer. They are of an elongated pyriform shape, and are so large and closely packed as to fill up entirely, in most cases, the spaces between the septa. In one or two of the compartments, however, a small space appears near the middle, the cells radiating towards it in all directions from the septa, body-wall, and œsophagus. These spaces constantly increase in size as development proceeds, and form the radiating chambers which surround the stomach. The cells are so closely packed at first that a longitudinal section in nearly any plane gives the appearance of fig. 136, the entoderm having the appearance simply of being greatly thickened in the oral region.

Anteriorly the septa extend quite across the gastric cavity from the œsophagus to the body-wall, as shown in the figure. Behind the œsophagus their inner edges are free and the septa appear in transverse section as low ridges which scarcely rise above the level of the general layer of entoderm. They may, however, be readily recognised by the presence of the central layer of supporting lamella and the radiating disposition of the cells over them. This is shown in fig. 143, which represents a section from the same larva (forty-eight hours) with fig. 142 taken farther back at the lower end of the œsophagus. Three of the septa still reach the œsophagus (x.), two are barely united with it, and two are separated from it by considerable intervals. As development proceeds the septa become constantly thinner and the intervening chambers increase correspondingly in size. This is effected partly through the increasing size of the larva and in part by a change of form in the entoderm cells covering the septa, which become far less elongated. Fig. 144 represents a section through the anterior part of a four days' larva in which the radiating chambers have attained a considerable size. Fig. 145 is from the same specimen at the posterior end of the œsophagus ; this corresponds very closely with the earlier stage shown in fig. 143. Fig. 146 is from the same specimen still further back, showing the free septa. The bilateral arrangement of the septa is strikingly shown in the symmetrical disposition of the septa of different widths (see p. 764). The entoderm cells have entirely changed their form, being now more or less flattened, or even forming in some places a flat pavement epithelium. On the edges of the septa have appeared the mesenterial filaments ($f.f.$) but a description of these may conveniently be deferred to the following section.

I have studied carefully the young septa for evidence of the participation of the ectoderm in their formation, but am led to conclude that they are formed almost exclusively from the entoderm, though in some cases a few ectoderm cells may make their way into the outer parts of the septa. In the youngest septa observed, the supporting lamella almost always appears as a simple membrane joining the lamella of the body-wall nearly at a right angle, and sometimes without interrupting its outline (fig. 147). In most cases, however, the lamella of the body-wall bends inwards slightly at the point where the septum meets it, and ectoderm cells with conspicuous nuclei may sometimes be seen lying directly in the angle thus formed (fig. 148.) (This figure is from the peduncular septum, but answers equally well for the radial septa.) In a very few cases the lamella appears to be actually infolded to some extent at the base of the septum, and ectoderm cells pass into the space thus formed, and thus come to lie within the body of the septum. In still other cases this fold appears to close up, forming a small triangular space at the root of the septum in which one or two ectoderm cells appear, as shown in fig. 149, *n*. These never extend far out into the septum, however, and the greater portion of the lamella of the latter is secreted, as I believe, by the bases of the entoderm cells.

The question as to whether the lamella of the septum is double, and contains ectoderm cells invaginated from the exterior, is one of much theoretical interest, since, if this be the case, the septa are to be regarded as actual infoldings of the entire body-wall, and not as simple entodermic ridges. LACAZE-DUTHIERS in his beautiful memoirs on the development of polyps,[*] expressly states that both of the layers of the body-wall participate in the formation of the septa, and he figures in the larvæ of *Astroides calycularis* ectoderm cells with numerous nematocysts passing directly into the body of the septum. On the other hand, he is strenuously opposed by KOWALEVSKY, who maintains that the entoderm alone is concerned in the formation of the septum. My own observations throw no new light on this interesting question; for although the great bulk of the septum with its lamella is in *Renilla* certainly entodermic, yet the occasional entrance of a few ectoderm cells into the base of the septum may indicate that an invagination of ectoderm originally occurred, in connexion with a special development of the underlying entoderm, but was subsequently nearly or completely lost. The matter is certainly worth further investigation in other polyps, for it is difficult to believe that LACAZE-DUTHIERS's figures rest upon no other basis than pure imagination.

b. Arrangement of the septa.

The septa are grouped about the œsophagus with a definite relation to the dorso-ventral axis, as shown in transverse sections (fig. 142). The cavity of the œsophagus is elongated in the dorso-ventral axis, and its angles are opposite two compartments, which may in KÖLLIKER's terminology be called the dorsal and ventral chambers. On each side of the œsophagus are, therefore, three chambers which are called respectively the dorso-lateral, median lateral or simply lateral, and ventro-lateral chambers. Following the same terminology, the septa may be designated as dorsal, dorso-lateral, ventro-lateral and ventral, respectively, there being four on each side of the œsophagus.

This bilateral grouping of the septa becomes very conspicuous in transverse sections

---

[*] Arch. de Zool. Exp. et Génér, tome i., ii.

below the œsophagus in later stages. In the four days' larva (fig. 146) the septa are clearly seen to be arranged in pairs on opposite sides of the dorso-ventral axis. The dorsal septa (*d.s.*) are very narrow and widely separated, and have no mesenterial filaments on their edges, the dorso-lateral (*d.l.s.*) are much wider, and are thickened at their edges to form the mesenterial filaments; the ventro-lateral septa (*v.l.s.*) are widest of all, and the ventral septa (*v.s.*) are about equal to the dorso-lateral.

When the septa are sufficiently far advanced to be visible from the exterior upon rendering the larva transparent by reagents or by compression in the fresh state, they are found to have a remarkable and definite arrangement. This arrangement is apparent at a very early stage, and remains unchanged as far as the development can be followed. Hence it will be convenient to describe it from a somewhat older specimen (figs. 103, 104, four days). The dorsal septa (*d.s.*) extend backwards for about one-fourth the length of the body, where they are joined by the dorso-lateral septa (*d.l.s.*). From their point of union the peduncular septum (*p.s.*) extends backwards to the aboral end of the body. The ventro-lateral septa (*v.l.s.*) extend backwards some distance beyond the point of union of the above-mentioned septa, and then bend upwards to join the peduncular septum at the point *u* (fig. 104). In some cases it is difficult to trace the septum up to the peduncular septum, especially when the larva is fully expanded. In fact, I completely overlooked their connexion in my earlier paper, and described the septum as terminating freely below. In some specimens this appears to be actually the case, though it is difficult to make sure of it, but in every case the line of longitudinal muscles accompanying the septum (see p. 780) is continued up to the peduncular septum. The ventral septa (*v.s.*) are of nearly the same length as the dorsal, and in some specimens appear to terminate freely below. In most cases, however, careful examination during a half-contracted state of the larva shows that the lower ends of the septa bend towards one another and unite in the median ventral line. From their point of union a band of longitudinal muscles extends backwards in the median line of the body. In specimens where the septa themselves do not actually join, the lines of accompanying muscles bend towards one another and unite in the same way that those of the ventro-lateral septa join the peduncular septum.

The arrangement of the septa shows, therefore, a very marked bilateral symmetry, the septa being disposed according to their width, length, and relations to each other, in pairs which are symmetrically placed with reference to the dorso-ventral plane.

c. *Formation of the peduncular septum.*

The peduncular septum has a quite different mode of origin from the radial septa, though it is continuous with the latter at their earliest appearance. It makes its appearance at about the fortieth hour at the *posterior* end of the body, sometimes, at any rate, before the stomodæum or the radial septa are formed. A longitudinal section through this part of the body of a forty-hour larva is shown in fig. 150. The rudiment of the peduncular septum (*p.s.*) appears as a rounded mass of entoderm cells, at the base of which is a delicate supporting lamella running inwards from the lamella of the body-wall, and becoming insensibly lost among the cells. The anterior part of the stomach still contains a considerable quantity of unabsorbed yolk, and the stomodæum is just beginning to be formed. From this point the septum grows rapidly forwards, ending by a free edge in front. As the septum extends forwards its lateral portions grow more rapidly than the middle, so that the free edge becomes deeply concave in front. I have no figures of this in early stages where it is most pronounced ; it is shown in fig. 136 at *e*, where it has extended very far forwards.

By reason of this structure of the septum, the posterior part of the body is completely divided into a dorsal and ventral chamber (fig. 154) ; while farther forwards, in front of the edge of the septum, the gastric cavity is undivided, and a section shows only the lateral forward extensions of the septum (fig. 154, *a.*, *a.*). These have exactly the appearance of two independent septa, situated on opposite sides of the body. If they be traced forwards they are found to be continuous with the dorsal septa at their point of union with the dorso-lateral pair, as explained at p. 765. The free edge gradually extends forwards until it reaches the point at which the lateral portions join the radial septa, and then remains stationary for a long period. Its subsequent development is described at p. 795.

A transverse section through the peduncular septum behind its free edge (fig. 151) shows that it is composed mainly of two thick layers of clear, rather ill-defined entoderm cells, separated by a peculiar membrane (*ax.*). At the sides this membrane appears like the ordinary lamella of the septa, and joins the lamella of the body-wall. Towards the middle, however, the membrane splits into two layers enclosing a narrow space in which appear numbers of conspicuous nuclei similar to those of the entoderm cells. Cell-outlines can only faintly be distinguished, but there can be no doubt that the nuclei belong to cells which are enclosed in the lamella and may conveniently be termed the *axial cells*. These cells are confined to the central portion of the septum behind the free edge. The forward extension of the lateral parts of the septum show no trace of anything like the axial cells in their lamella. As development proceeds, the axial cells become more and more flattened between the enclosing layers of lamella and at length nearly or quite disappear (fig. 173, *p.s.*). The lamella of the peduncular septum has then the same appearance as that of the radial septa in which no axial cells were ever observed.

In order to ascertain the origin of the axial cells it is necessary to study sections of still earlier stages of development. Fig. 153 represents a longitudinal section of a somewhat younger larva (forty-eight hours). The entoderm cells forming the main mass of the septum are here very distinct and of a high columnar form. The axial cells are larger and their outlines are more distinct. Their appearance is more clearly shown in fig. 136, from another specimen. The lamella is simple behind but splits further forwards into two delicate membranes between which lie the axial cells. The latter are clear, with very delicate, rounded or polygonal outlines, and with very conspicuous intensely stained nuclei, which are quite similar to those of the entoderm cells (*en*.). Towards the free edge of the septum (*e*.) the two layers of the lamella disappear and the axial cells become confounded with the entoderm cells.

The latter point is most clearly shown in transverse sections taken just behind the free edge of the septum (fig. 152). We find here that the lamella of the lateral portion is simple as in the radial septa, but further inwards the lamella splits into two layers between which lie a number of closely packed axial cells. Still farther inwards the layers of the lamella entirely disappear and the axial cells graduate insensibly into the rounded entoderm cells which form the edge of the septum. In the section immediately behind this, the layer of axial cells can be traced quite across from one side to the other, but they lie several cells thick in the middle and are scarcely distinguishable from the adjoining entoderm cells. In sections further forwards the septum entirely disappears and the body of the larva consists of an unbroken layer of ectoderm and entoderm enclosing a nearly solid mass of yolk.

These sections show very clearly that as the septum grows forwards the entoderm cells of which it is composed arrange themselves in three layers. The two outer layers persist as the entodermic covering of the peduncular septum, and form its main bulk ; the cells of the middle layer atrophy, flatten together, and form the axial cells. The two layers of lamella which enclose the axial cells are no doubt secreted by the adjoining entoderm cells ; the appearances indicate that these membranes are simply the confluent and much thickened membranes of the cells.

As in the case of the radial septa, I have studied with care the possibility of ectodermic cells passing into the septum at its lateral parts where it joins the body-wall, but have been unable to find decisive evidence of such a process. The sections show exactly the same appearances as those of the radial septa. The lamella of the septum sometimes joins that of the body-wall abruptly, without any infolding of the latter; in other cases the lamella of the body-wall is somewhat infolded, and the angle thus formed contains ectoderm cells; in other cases, again, a small triangular space appears at the root of the septum, enclosing one or two cells. The latter are quite similar to the ectoderm cells which appear in the last-described case, and seem to have been introduced from the outside. In rare cases, one of which is carefully represented in fig. 156, the lamella has the appearance of folding in so as to leave a narrow connexion between the cleft containing the axial cells and the ectodermic layer. From these appearances I conclude that the ectoderm cells may in some cases actually pass into the septum by an infolding of the lamella, but they can never do so in considerable numbers, and take only the most insignificant part in the formation of the septum. Far the greater part of the peduncular septum, as of the radial septa, is formed from entoderm cells alone. Misled by certain theoretical considerations, I was at first strongly inclined to regard the axial cells as ectodermic in origin, having been invaginated from the exterior in a fold of the lamella. More careful study entirely disproved this view. The entodermic origin of the axial cells is placed beyond all doubt, by the fact that typical entodermic spicules are sometimes developed in them. These are unmistakable in form and optical characters, and are never developed in ectoderm cells.

In its earlier stages the peduncular septum forms a complete partition, extending from side to side, and reaching the posterior end of the body. At a later period it becomes perforated along its sides, and at its posterior extremity by rounded openings, which place the chambers of the peduncle in communication. The posterior opening (fig. 155, *p.*) becomes very large, and the lateral openings (*o.*) also increase in size, until the septum has the appearance of being suspended by narrow threads from the lateral walls of the peduncle (see figs. 181, 182). The lateral openings subsequently become much reduced in size, or even close entirely (figs. 206, 207), but the posterior opening remains permanently in the adult, and has been described and figured by KÖLLIKER.

In *Leptogorgia* the eight radial septa are visible when the larva ceases to swim, and attaches itself to the bottom (fig. 113). So far as could be determined, they develop simultaneously, and extend throughout the entire length of the body, without joining one another, or otherwise departing from a strictly radial disposition. They have, however, the same bilateral arrangement with respect to the œsophagus as in *Renilla*. The mouth and œsophagial cavity are distinctly elongated in a definite plane, which may by analogy be regarded as the dorso-ventral. Nothing like the peduncular septum in its fully formed condition was observed, but there is an accumulation of entoderm cells at the aboral end of the larva (fig. 116), developed in connexion with the axis, which is very similar to the peduncular septum in its earliest stages.

Review.

The radial septa and the peduncular septum are structures widely different from one another in structure and origin. The former have a simple cuticular supporting lamella, consist of two strata of entoderm cells, arise at the anterior extremity of the body and grow backwards; the latter, on the other hand, has a double supporting lamella, consists of three layers of entoderm cells, arises at the posterior end of the body and grows forwards.

The eight radial septa are of universal occurrence among the *Alcyonaria*, have in all cases the same grouping about the œsophagus, possess an entirely similar musculature, and for these reasons are clearly homologous throughout the group. I had strong hopes that a careful study of the early development of the radial septa might give some indication of the relation in which they stand to the septa of other groups of polyps. The result is, however, a purely negative one, and affords absolutely no new basis for speculation upon the systematic affinities of the *Alcyonaria*. Their development is greatly condensed and abbreviated, and shows not the slightest indication of any such remarkable and regular sequence as that which LACAZE-DUTHIERS has shown to characterise the development of the septa in various representatives of the Zoantharia.* In this respect *Renilla* agrees with all the Alcyonaria whose embryonic development has been investigated, though observations on this matter are so scanty as to afford no satisfactory basis for comparison. In the case of *Alcyonium*, KOWALEVSKY was unable to make out the succession of the septa, but he states that it seemed to be analogous to that of the Zoantharia, as described by LACAZE-DUTHIERS. This statement is, however, too vague to be of any value.

The lateral forward extensions of the peduncular septum (fig. 154) have precisely the same structure as the ordinary septa, and they are continuous anteriorly with the dorsal pair of septa. Hence there can be little doubt that the peduncular septum is to be regarded as formed by the union of the dorsal pair of radial septa, beginning at the posterior end and extending thence forwards. It is highly probable that all of the septa in *Renilla* originally extended to the posterior extremity of the body; for this is the case in the larval *Leptogorgia* and in nearly all other polyps (*Cerianthus* excepted). The six ventral septa have ceased to extend as far as the posterior extremity, but the primitive condition has been retained by the dorsal septa and they have furthermore united by their inner edges to form a flat plate, the peduncular septum

The axial cells, according to this view, are to be regarded as having been formed along the line of union between the two septa by a peculiar arrangement of the entoderm cells in this region (see fig. 152). Before considering the cause of such an arrangement, it is necessary to look for the homologue of the peduncular septum in other Pennatulids. As has already been stated, no homologous structure is known to exist, except in the Pennatulacea; but its homologies in this group appear tolerably clear although they cannot be determined with certainty without further embryological investigation. KÖLLIKER has described with great care the structure of the peduncle in many species of Pennatulids. The most usual and typical structure is as follows. The cavity of the peduncle is divided by four septa into four chambers of which two occupy a lateral position, the third is dorsal, and the fourth ventral. The four septa meet in the middle of the peduncular cavity, forming a central mass within which lies the axis enclosed in an epithelial sheath. Toward the posterior end the two lower septa become free from the body walls and run out upon the hinder end of the axis which lies free in the peduncular cavity. A part of each upper septum likewise extends out upon the free extremity of the axis, but the remaining parts of the upper septa fuse together to form a single transverse septum which runs backwards to the tip of the peduncle and thus divides the latter at its posterior end into a dorsal and a ventral chamber. (For a full description of this very peculiar arrangement, which can scarcely be described without figures, see KÖLLIKER's 'Pennatuliden,' p. 23).

* Arch. d. Zool. Exp., tome i., ii.

What the relation of these four septa is to the axial polyp is quite unknown, owing to the complete lack of anatomical studies of very young Pennatulids. Through what process the lower end of the axis comes to lie free in the peduncular cavity is also unknown. But it seems highly probable, as KÖLLIKER remarks (*l.c.*, p. 270) that the peduncular septum of *Renilla* is homologous with the single horizontal septum (*septum transversale* of KÖLLIKER) of the posterior part of the peduncle in other Pennatulids. This homology appears especially clear in the case of *Renilla amethystina* (VERRILL) ; for in this case, the extreme anterior part of the peduncle is divided as in the Pennatulidæ into four chambers, which clearly correspond to the four longitudinal canals of the latter. A section through this part of the peduncle (which is situated near its anterior end and forms in reality a part of the disc) is very similar except in the lack of an axis to a section through the four chambers of *Pennatula* (see fig. 72, plate 8, KÖLLIKER). The two additional chambers of *Renilla amethystina* are laterally placed, and are developed apparently as a pair of cavities in the substance of the peduncular septum. The four partitions which thus arise are all continuous behind with the single horizontal septum.

This comparison appears to me to be well founded, though it cannot be proved so without the aid of further embryological studies. If it is so, *Renilla amethystina* is a perfect connecting link, so far as the structure of the peduncle goes, between *R. reniformis* and the axis-bearing Pennatulids.

In all the latter forms the axis, when present, is suspended by these four septa, and it is difficult to understand their appearance in *Renilla amethystina*, except on the supposition that in this form an axis once existed, but was subsequently lost. In *R. reniformis*, the four septa also have disappeared, leaving only the peduncular septum as the representative of the *septum transversale*. This view is supported by the development of the colony which, as pointed out in section 19, indicates the derivation of *Renilla* from an axis-bearing form, resembling the *Bathyptileœ*.

As a matter of fact, we find the axis developed in very different degrees in the various genera of the Pennatulids ; and in certain of the *Veretillidœ*, as *Clavella* or *Cavernularia*, the axis is very small or, even in some species of the same genera, quite absent. Whether the rudimentary condition or total want of an axis in these forms is due to the gradual loss of an axis cannot be determined ; but the probabilities certainly appear to be in favour of such a view, since these genera have a much less primitive structure in some other respects than some of the axis-bearing forms. We are perhaps able to get some idea of how the axis might be gradually lost. Since the axis ends at some distance from the tip of the peduncle, a certain amount of movement is still permitted to the latter ; and the great development of the peduncular muscles indicates that this power of movement must be an important factor in the life of the organism. In *Renilla* the power of movement is of vital importance (see p. 784), and an axis would be of no conceivable use. It is easily conceivable that the power of movement might become of paramount importance to one of the axis-bearing forms, and the presence of a rigid axis would in such a case be disadvantageous. Hence we can see how, by natural selection, the posterior muscular part of the peduncle might be constantly increased in size and importance, accompanied by a corresponding reduction of the axis. If this process were continued until the axis disappeared, a condition would result like that shown in *Renilla amethystina*, and by a further reduction the structure of *R. reniformis* would be attained, in which the dorsal and ventral chambers and the *septum transversale* alone remained.

The foregoing considerations strongly suggest that the peculiarities in the structure and formation of the peduncular septum may be in some way a result of the former existence of an axis. It is, however, useless to speculate on this matter so long as the development of the axis in the typical Pennatulids is unknown; and in regard to this, in KÖLLIKER's words, "mangeln alle und jede Erfahrungen."

Two entirely different views of the Pennatulid axis have been entertained. KÖLLIKER, on the one hand, regards it as of mesodermic origin, the mesodermic elements being supposed to be originally derived from the entoderm. To quote his own words ('Pennatuliden,' p. 428): "Anders bei der Kalkaxe, denn hier spielt ein osteoblastenähnliche Zellenlage, deren Abstammung von dem Entoderma zwar wohl sicher vermuthet werden darf, aber noch nicht nachgewiesen ist, eine Hauptrolle." On the other hand, KOCH considers the axis as probably ectodermic in its origin. This author, while admitting the so-called axis of a certain division of the Gorgonacea (Pseudaxonia) to be mesodermic, has given very strong reasons for the belief that the true axis of many Alcyonaria is secreted by a layer of epithelial cells directly derived from the ectoderm. KÖLLIKER himself observed that in some of the Pennatulida (*Pteroides, Virgularia*) the axis is surrounded by a distinct epithelial layer, and KOCH has shown that this is the case not only in other Pennatulacea, but also in those Gorgonida which possess a true axis. KOCH's observations are conclusive that this epithelial layer, in the fixed Gorgonians, consists of invaginated ectoderm cells which secrete the axis as a cuticular structure. This "axis-epithelium" of the fixed Gorgonians is identical in structure with that of the Pennatulids, and the latter is believed by KOCH, though from analogy only, to be also ectodermic, its original connexion with the exterior having been lost.

In the face of such conflicting views as to the nature of the axis, it is impossible to determine its real relation to the peduncular septa and the *septum transversale*. Without definite knowledge on this point, it is clearly premature to frame any definite hypothesis as to the significance of the peduncular septum of *Renilla*, and the solution of this problem can only be found by studying the embryology of the axis-bearing Pennatulids.

§ 10. *Development of the mesenterial filaments.*

The mesenterial filaments are visible as soon as the larva becomes sufficiently transparent as dark granular thickenings on the edges of the septa at their upper portions where they join the œsophagus. They may be seen while the larva is still swimming, but their arrangement can be made out only after the larva has attached itself and the body has begun to elongate. It is then apparent that they vary in length and have a definite disposition. Those of the dorsal septa are very short indeed (fig. 177), or in some cases may not be visible at all when the others are well developed. They appear as knob-like prolongations of the lip of the œsophagus attached to edges of the dorsal septa. The dorso-lateral filaments (*d.l.f.*) are much longer, extending along the edges of the septa nearly to the buds (*p¹.*) which have now appeared at the point where the dorsal and dorso-lateral septa unite. The ventro-lateral filaments (*v.l.f.*) are still longer and extend down to the level of the buds or beyond them. The ventral filaments, finally, are very short, being intermediate in length between the dorsal and dorso-lateral filaments.

This grouping of the filaments is quite constant and exists at a very early stage. It is extremely difficult to determine whether these varying lengths represent the actual succession of the filaments since the latter are in their early stages closely contracted together and their arrangement cannot be made out. This grouping persists for a long time and the dorsal filaments remain permanently shorter than the others, and of different structure as KÖLLIKER has observed. (The dorsal filaments are in many cases longer than the others, but this is, in *Renilla* at least, only apparent, and is due to the fact that they never become convoluted like those of the lateral and ventral septa.) All of the filaments except the dorsal pair increase rapidly in length and very soon become folded back and forth and variously convoluted (see figs. 183, 205). This is a result of the circumstance that the filaments increase in length much more rapidly than the septa which bear them, and they are necessarily therefore thrown into folds or "gathers."

The dorsal filaments grow backwards very slowly and are never thrown into transverse folds (see figs. 183, 204). They are less opaque than the other filaments, with a darker central line, and are of much less diameter than the others. These differences are permanent and persist in the adult. The dorsal filaments always remain in connexion with the œsophagus, and appear like long narrow prolongations of the latter down upon the edges of the septa. The other filaments, though at first extending quite up to the œsophagus, soon become more or less widely separated from the œsophagus, fading insensibly away a short distance below the lips of the latter.

In transverse sections the filaments appear as simple thickenings of the entoderm at the edges of the septa, which differ in appearance from the remaining entoderm of the septa only in being more granular. The supporting lamella may be traced out nearly to the middle of the thickening where it fades away and disappears.

The filaments appear to arise near the lips of the œsophagus, growing thence downwards along the septa. This suggests the possibility of ectodermic elements from the stomodæum entering into their composition, and I have made many longitudinal sections for the study of this point. Fig. 157 represents a longitudinal section through a larva of 100 hours (the mouth being fully formed) and the remains of the œsophageal plug (probably) being attached to a septum at *pl*. To the left is a mesenterial filament (*f.*) clearly outlined and well differentiated from the rest of the septum by its more intense colour and granular appearance. Above, the ectoderm of the stomodæum may be very clearly distinguished from the entoderm by its less granular appearance and different colour. Following the ectoderm of the stomodæum downwards, it passes insensibly into the entoderm of the filament without any indication of a limit between them. On the right side, however, the ectoderm is separated below by a faint rounded outline, below which the entoderm is slightly thickened and more granular. The large granular mass is possibly a filament but more probably the œsophageal plug. The same general features are shown in fig. 158, and the ectoderm at the left side of the stomodæum becomes entirely continuous below with the entoderm of a mesenterial filament (*f.*).

From these sections it might be concluded that the filaments are actually downgrowths from the stomodæum. In some cases, however, the filament appears to have at first no connexion with the œsophagus. This is shown for instance in fig. 159, where the filament (*f.*) on the left side ends in front by a definite rounded outline and has no connexion with the œsophagus. It is possible that this thickening on the septum is not really a filament but a part of the œsophageal plug. Nearly conclusive evidence is however afforded by the section shown in fig. 137. In this specimen there is a thickening on the edge of a septum (*f.*) which is probably the beginning of a mesenterial filament before the cavity of the œsophagus has broken through, and there is no possibility of any communication with the stomodæal ectoderm.

In *Leptogorgia* the filaments become visible shortly after the attachment of the larva. Two of them are much shorter than the others and are borne by a pair of septa which enclose one of the chambers at the angles of the elongated mouth ; they are in all probability homologous with the dorsal pair of filaments in *Renilla*. The six other filaments are much longer and are equal to one another in length. This arrangement was maintained almost unchanged for seven weeks when the young polyps were killed.

Conclusions.

The mesenterial filaments are at first purely entodermic structures, formed as thickenings on the edges of the septa. After the absorption of the bottom of the œsophagus the ectoderm of the stomodæum becomes directly continuous with the entoderm of the edges of the septa and mesenterial filaments. Hence the possibility certainly exists of the filaments or septa containing elements derived from the ectoderm. This must be borne in mind in considering the origin of the sexual elements which subsequently make their appearance in the walls of the dorso-lateral and ventro-lateral septa ; for their derivation from the ectoderm is brought within the bounds of possibility. All writers agree that both ova and spermatozoa in the Anthozoa are derived from entoderm, and this has usually been regarded as beyond all question. The probabilities certainly appear to be very strongly in favour of this view, but it must, I think, be admitted that the possibility of an ectodermic origin for the sexual elements is not entirely excluded. [See Appendix.]

§ 11. *Changes of external form, appearance of the tentacles, and general histological changes.*

When the larva abandons its free-swimming life and settles upon the bottom it has a more or less elongated form, and the posterior part of the body is very extensible and changeable in shape. The ectoderm and entoderm have undergone little change. The entoderm cells are large and clear, with scanty coarse granules, and very distinct large oval nuclei. The ectoderm cells still retain their high columnar form, and have a finely granular contents, which stains slightly. The cells are planted on the lamella, and many of them extend through the entire thickness of the ectoderm. Besides the columnar form, there are other more or less rounded cells in the deeper layers of the ectoderm.

The body now elongates rapidly (figs. 176–178), and the ectoderm undergoes a great change. The columnar cells lose their form, become rounded, proliferate rapidly, and lose their connexion with the lamella. The outermost cells finally become flattened or fusiform, and form a thin layer covering the exterior of the body (see figs. 173–175). At the same time a considerable amount of clear gelatinous matter is formed, which sometimes entirely separates the cells from each other (figs. 160, 161), and forms the greater part of the ectoderm. In the deeper parts of the ectoderm appear rounded cells of various forms. Here and there are very large, deeply-stained, oval cells (fig. 166, *sp.*) ; others are nearly spherical, and groups of four deeply-stained cells are occasionally seen (fig. 166). Besides these, long fusiform cells may in some places be seen lying on the outer side of the lamella. These characters appear especially in the middle and posterior parts of the body. In the anterior region transitional forms may be seen, and at the extreme anterior end the columnar form is long retained.

The entoderm cells undergo meanwhile little change ; they vary greatly in appearance according to the state of contraction of the body. During contraction they are of a high columnar form but when the body is fully extended they become much shortened or even flattened.

Leptogorgia presents the same general histological characters at this stage but the ectoderm cells at the aboral end by which the larva attaches itself retain a high columnar form and very granular structure, and secrete a yellowish cement by which the young polyp is firmly attached. The entoderm is also much thickened at this point. This thickening of the layers is shown at α, in figs. 115 to 117. The cement substance is undoubtedly to be regarded as the first rudiment of the axis, which is therefore an ectodermic product. It is probable that budding takes place from the basal part of the young polyp so that the colony has at first the form of a flattened plate or encrustation covering the object to which it is attached by the cement secreted by the bases of the polyps. This may be inferred from the structure of the adult colony, but I did not succeed in observing the budding in young stages although the young polyps were kept for seven weeks in the aquarium. The individual shown in figs. 115 to 117 did not attach itself, and the thickening of the layers at the base was much greater than in those which became attached. Upon making a longitudinal section through this specimen, when seven weeks old, the dark mass, α, was found to contain a solid yellow horny mass composed of a substance quite like the cement by which other individuals were attached. The basal part of the wall of the body seems to have been invaginated and the cement then secreted in the cavity thus formed. The polyp therefore appeared to have an internal axis, but this must be regarded as an unusual condition which probably occurs only when the larva fails to attach itself.

The tentacles, in both genera, appear soon after the attachment of the larva as conical outgrowths from the anterior ends of the radial chambers (figs. 115 and 176). I have not observed the least difference in the time of their appearance though I have observed them in every stage of development and in many different individuals. In this respect, as in the formation of the septa, the development of the Alcyonaria is more abbreviated than that of the Zoantharia; for in many representatives of the latter group the tentacles, like the septa, develop in regular sequence.

The tentacles are at first quite simple, with no indication of pinnæ. The latter soon make their appearance along the sides of the tentacles, a new pair being formed, roughly speaking, every day. The new pinnæ are formed near the base of the tentacle and are carried outwards by the longitudinal growth of the latter. The formation of pinnæ ceases after about ten to twelve pairs have appeared and the growth of the tentacles is arrested. The pinnæ are somewhat irregularly disposed and the paired arrangement often disappears towards the tip of the tentacle. Those in the middle of the tentacle are always longer than the basal or apical ones. The pinnæ are formed as simple diverticula from the tentacle and consist accordingly of a layer of ectoderm and entoderm separated by the lamella and enclosing a prolongation from the cavity of the tentacle. The tips of the tentacles and pinnæ are often slightly swollen from the accumulation of minute thread-cells at these points.

§ 12. *Development of the spicules and calyx-teeth.*

The spicules of *Renilla*, as EISEN observed, are of two different forms, and I have found these to have an entirely different origin. The large elongated spicules which give the colony its beautiful purple colour and stiffen its walls are produced entirely by the ectoderm. On the other hand the small transparent oval spicules, which occur in small numbers only, are developed in the entoderm alone.

The former make their appearance soon after the attachment of the larva on each side of the middle region of the body near the first pair of buds. They have the appearance of delicate transparent rod-like bodies which are at first quite colourless. They increase slowly in number, extending backward along the line of the peduncular septum on each side. It is only when the formation of the colony is well advanced that they acquire a purple colour and begin to extend forwards towards the oral extremity and upwards and downwards around the body. They gradually extend over the whole area of the body which therefore acquires a delicate purple tint, except towards the tip of the peduncle which remains white. The spicules become very scanty or quite disappear towards the anterior extremity and assume a peculiar arrangement at their upper limit. In each compartment some distance behind the bases of the tentacles they arrange themselves in lines radiating backward and sidewise from a small central area which ultimately forms the tip of a calyx-tooth (fig. 185, *cx.*). At the same time this region becomes elevated so as to form a low conical prominence which in later stages gradually grows out into a hollow pointed diverticulum from the chamber, its walls being stiffened by long spicules; this is a calyx-tooth. When the crown of tentacles is retracted the tooth lies at the anterior end and forms a hard pointed prominence projecting forwards. Calyx-teeth appear on all of the chambers except the ventral one where the formation of a tooth is a rare exception.

In transverse sections the needle-shaped spicules are found to lie in the lower layers of the ectoderm outside the lamella, and a study of the smallest spicules shows that they are formed in the interior of rounded cells lying in the ectoderm. It is difficult to demonstrate the spicule-cells, even in the earliest stages of the spicules, and I have never seen them with certainty after the spicules have attained any considerable size. They cannot be isolated by teasing, and when *in situ* it is difficult to distinguish them from the surrounding cells. By staining the tissues deeply with eosin the bodies of the cells may occasionally be clearly distinguished. Figs. 171ᵃ to 171ᵍ show different forms of the cells containing very young spicules. In some of the cells nuclei appear; in others they are invisible. The calcareous matter first appears as an irregular elongated mass in the protoplasm of the cell and shows to the eye no trace of crystalline structure. As a rule there is only a single concretion in a cell, but the spicules are occasionally formed from two centres, as in fig. 171ᵉ. As the spicule increases in size the enclosing layer of protoplasm becomes very thin and I have never been able to demonstrate it in spicules of one-fourth the full size. The largest spicule figured (g.) is not more than one-eighth the length of a fully formed spicule.

The entodermic spicules (figs. 172^d to 172^a) make their appearance at a much earlier period than those of the ectoderm. They first appear in the lateral portions of the peduncular septum as oval, highly refractive bodies, which are plainly visible from the exterior (fig. 181). They become in time very numerous and are arranged in an irregular longitudinal band on each side of the septum. They appear also in the entoderm of the lateral walls of the body and are especially numerous near the posterior end. They become easily detached from their points of origin and may often be seen suspended in the fluid which circulates in the cavities of the young polyp. Most of the spicules of the peduncular septum are formed in its two outer layers, but it often happens that a few are developed in the axial cells and when the latter atrophy are left embedded in the lamella (see p. 766).

The entodermic spicules also are formed in the interior of cells which may much more readily be demonstrated than the ectodermic spicule-cells. The cells, as shown in fig. 172, are variable in form and usually contain distinct nuclei. The calcareous matter is first deposited in the form of very minute rounded nodules which, as in the case of the ectoderm spicules, may be clearly brought into view by examination with polarised light. Examined by ordinary transmitted light they appear in their earliest stages as transparent, scarcely visible bodies: or they may be quite invisible. If, however, they be examined with the polariser, and the upper prism be rotated, they come into view with the greatest clearness; and by a proper adjustment of the prisms both the cell and the calcareous nodules come clearly into view. The spicule-cells may contain only one nodule, or two or three may be present. In the latter case each nodule appears in some cases to give rise to an independent spicule. In other cases spicules may be seen more or less closely united in groups of two, three, or four, and it is probable that each such group is developed within a single cell. The form of the nodules varies exceedingly, being spherical, oval, or irregularly angular. A not uncommon appearance is shown in fig. 172^a. The spicule has an oval form and its substance refracts the light in such a way as to produce two darker lozenge-shaped areas at the ends. The fully formed spicules are usually of a smoothly rounded oval form but are in many cases obscurely angular at the ends (see figs. 172^a). This is not definite enough, however, to admit of comparison with inorganic crystals.

If the spicules be treated with dilute acid, the calcareous matter is dissolved with effervescence, leaving a nearly transparent organic basis which accurately retains the form of the spicules. In some cases, at least, their organic basis is formed before the calcareous matter is deposited. I have sometimes seen cells resembling the spicule-cells, and containing clear bodies quite similar to the calcareous nodules, but destitute of calcareous matter.

In order to determine the molecular structure of the spicules, I submitted a number of them to Professor B. K. EMERSON, the well-known mineralogist of Amherst

College, for examination with the polariscope. He kindly undertook to examine them, and the following statement of his results is quoted verbatim :—

"I find the smaller spicules to polarise perfectly and very brightly, and if the spicules are a carbonate, it is probably aragonite rather than calcite, because of the bright colour it affords.

"Each spicule is made up of a core of crystalline material surrounded by a thin layer of non-polarising matter, and this by an outer layer, slightly thicker, and also of equal thickness, which polarises as does the core.

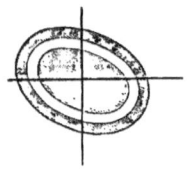

"The crystalline axes uniformly run parallel to the long and short diagonals, as in the sketch, so that the core is a crystal probably of the rhombic system, and the outer layer is controlled in its position by this core and has parallel axes with it.

"The larger spicules I can best explain by saying that for a moment, on examining the slides, I supposed the small ones to be cross sections of the former (larger) ones. They are like bones filled with marrow under the microscope, the bone and the marrow representing the core and the outer layer of the small ones, and these being separated by an amorphous (in one case there were two amorphous layers) layer. In this case, the long axis of the spicule is a crystallographic axis. And bone and marrow are *orientirt* alike."

From this, the very interesting fact appears that the spicules are formed by a true process of crystallisation, though the form and structure of the crystals are modified, probably by reason of their deposition in an organic viscous medium. This point, as noted below, is one of much theoretical interest.

In *Leptogorgia* the characteristic spicules appear in the ectoderm soon after the attachment of the larva. They are quite irregularly distributed, and extend up into the bases of the tentacles. No entodermic spicules were observed.

Review.

My observations on the development of the spicules are in accord with those of KOWALEVSKY on the spicules of *Sympodium* (Zool. Anzeiger, No. 38, 1879), and as KOWALEVSKY points out, the process is quite similar to the formation of spicules in the mesoderm cells of sponges observed by SCHULTZE and METSCHNIKOFF. Their mode of development strongly recalls the formation of inorganic crystals in the interior of vegetable cells, and possibly indicates the origin of the spicular skeleton. This question presents serious difficulties under the theory of natural selection, for it is impossible to see how the occasional appearance of minute calcareous nodules in the tissues can originally have been of any use to the organism.

Everyone is familiar with the formation of crystals of lime salts in the interior of vegetable cells, where they perform no function as supporting organs, and are apparently mere by-products of the activity of the protoplasm. In this respect the entodermic spicules of *Renilla* resemble the deposits in many vegetable cells; for they are of no use to the colony as supporting organs, and unless we consider their present condition as having been acquired through degeneration, they must originally have been developed without reference to such a function. From the analogy of the deposits in vegetable cells, and in the entoderm cells of *Renilla*, it seems not improbable that the ectodermic spicules of *Renilla* had originally no function as supporting organs, having been formed simply as by-products of the activity of the protoplasm under peculiar conditions, such, for instance, as a superabundance of lime salts in the water. If, however, calcareous nodules once made their appearance in any considerable quantity in the tissues, they might serve as supporting organs, and be developed through natural selection to almost any extent. They might thus attain the great size and functional importance of the ectodermic spicules of *Renilla* or other Pennatulids, or by agglutination come to form a compact skeleton as in *Tubipora*.

It is remarkable to find so wide a difference between the skeletons of Alcyonaria and Zoantharia, as must exist if KOCH's recent conclusions as to the skeleton of *Asteroides calycularis* are well founded;[*] and it seems probable that the skeleton has been quite independently acquired in the two groups. The present considerations will, of course, apply to the Alcyonarian skeleton only.

§ 13. *Development of the muscular system.*

The larva of three days is very changeable in form (figs. 104, 105), showing that contractile elements have made their appearance; and careful examination of specimens rendered transparent by reagents reveals the presence of numerous short delicate unstriated muscle-fibres underlying the ectoderm. These are found to have a definite and constant arrangement, which will be described before considering the histology of the tissue.

a. *Distribution.*

The muscle-fibres are from the first arranged in two systems, viz.: a layer of longitudinal fibres, and a layer of circular fibres, which ultimately come to lie outside the former. The circular fibres first appear in the posterior half of the body in a broad

* Mittheilungen aus der Zool. Station zu Neapel, Band iii., Heft iii., 1882, pp. 284–292.

sheet which nearly encircles the body, but is interrupted at certain points where the longitudinal fibres are situated. As seen in surface view (figs. 160, 161 c.m.) they appear as delicate transparent fibres which are quite disconnected from one another. The sheet of circular fibres extends at first no further forwards than the first pair of buds ; but as development proceeds the fibres extend forwards to the oral extremity. In the tentacles they seem never to be developed.

The longitudinal fibres differ from the circular in being at first arranged in definite tracts. These correspond in part with the septa, a narrow band of fibres following the line of attachment of each of the radial septa, and of the peduncular septum on each side of the body ; these may be termed the septal tracts. Besides these there are two median tracts extending forwards, above and below, from the posterior extremity of the body. The dorsal median tract extends forwards nearly to the first pair of buds and there terminates. The ventral median tract bifurcates at its anterior extremity, and the two branches become continuous with the tracts of the ventral septa (see fig. 176 and p. 765). This arrangement of the longitudinal muscles is strongly bilateral, the median plane corresponding with the dorso-ventral axis of the body. From these primitive tracts the longitudinal fibres gradually extend laterally until they form an unbroken sheet lying within the circular fibres. They also extend forwards into the tentacles, and out towards their tips.

In transverse sections the longitudinal fibres appear as small dark spots lying in the basal part of the entoderm just within, and in contact with the supporting lamella. The entoderm cells covering the median tracts always show a fan-shaped arrangement, which is especially marked in younger stages, while the tract is still very narrow, as shown in fig. 162 (dorsal tract). Fig. 164 represents the ventral tract of a young specimen, and fig. 163 the same tract of an older individual.

The septal tracts (fig. 165) are divided into two parts by the lamella of the septum. In early stages these two parts lie at the base of the septum ; but as development proceeds the fibres on the *ventral* side gradually extend out into the septum, until at length they cover a broad tract on the ventral face of the lamella. They also extend for some distance out upon the ventral face of the peduncular septum (fig. 167). (The presence of longitudinal muscles in the lateral portions of the peduncular septum is mentioned by KÖLLIKER, ' Pennatuliden,' p. 274.) These muscles form the retractors of the polyp, which have therefore the arrangement characteristic of all the Alcyonarian polyps which have thus far been examined. (*Cf.* KÖLLIKER, EISEN, LINDAHL, MOSELEY, and HAACKE.)

The circular muscles can scarcely be seen in transverse sections, but are here and there visible, as in fig. 169. In longitudinal sections they are plainly visible (fig. 168) as a series of dark spots within the supporting lamella. They are somewhat irregularly placed, and are not grouped in definite tracts.

b. Histology.

By macerating the tissues in Hertwigs' mixture of osmic and acetic acids (see p. 728) the entodermic elements can be teased apart, and the muscle-cells completely isolated. We find thus that each muscle-fibre is developed from the base of an entoderm cell, the fibre and cell together constituting an "epithelio-muscular" cell or—to adopt the more convenient term proposed by Claus—a myoblast.

The myoblasts are of exceedingly diverse forms, as illustrated by the series of figures (170^d to 170^p). There is great variation in the length of the fibre, depending apparently on the age of the fibre, since the shorter ones are often no thicker than the longer.

The fibres taper towards both ends and are sometimes thrown into transverse folds. They consist of a homogeneous highly refractive substance which differs entirely from the body of the cell. The latter is composed of a granular substance, and contains a distinct rounded nucleus. As to the form of the cell, every gradation may be observed between a regular columnar cell planted on the fibre (fig. 170^d) and a slight accumulation of protoplasm surrounding a nucleus, which is closely applied to the side of the fibre (fig. 170^p). In all of the forms a delicate layer of granular protoplasm often extends for a considerable distance along the fibre (see figs. $170^{g, n, p}$).

From these appearances I conclude that the body of the cell always extends at first to the surface of the entoderm, the myoblast being at this stage a typical "epithelio-muscular" cell. As the fibre increases in size the body of the cell sinks into the entoderm and diminishes in size, the myoblast then becoming an "intra-epithelial" muscular cell (Hertwigs). Finally, the myoblast is wholly buried in the entoderm, the cell-body dwindles away and a "sub-epithelial" cell results—*i.e.*, an ordinary nucleated muscle-fibre. This course of development is, however, only inferred from the perfect series of forms shown among the myoblasts, since the outlines of the cells cannot be distinguished in the sections with sufficient clearness to follow their development.

The fibres of both layers are at first arranged in simple flat sheets. Later, the lamella is thrown into folds, so that both systems of muscles assume a more or less arborescent form in sections. The foldings take place in a very peculiar manner, such that those of the longitudinal layer alone are visible in transverse sections, and, *mutatis mutandis*, those of the circular layer in longitudinal sections. I have not followed in detail the development of these folds, since it has been very thoroughly studied by the Hertwig Brothers in the Actiniæ.

Review.

Both systems of muscles, circular and longitudinal, are formed in the entoderm alone, and an ectodermic musculature is entirely wanting, with the possible exception of some of the muscles of the tentacles. No other case of a purely entodermic musculature, so far as I am aware, is known to exist, though in most of the Actiniæ the ectodermal muscles are very feebly developed, as JOURDAN and the Brothers HERTWIG have shown. This result can, however, hardly occasion surprise, in view of the astonishing amount of variation in the musculature of polyps. KOWALEVSKY states that the longitudinal muscles of *Alcyonium* are of entodermic origin, but refers the circular muscles doubtfully to the ectoderm. Beyond these, observations on the embryonic development of the muscles in Alcyonaria are wanting.

In their mode of development the muscle-fibres agree with other Cœlenterata with exception of the Ctenophora. They are developed in the form of epithelio-muscular cells or myoblasts, which have the same form and structure as those of other Anthozoa, as described especially by the Brothers HERTWIG and by JOURDAN. The myoblasts do not, however, retain this form permanently, as is the case with many polyps. The cell-bodies become reduced to a small quantity of protoplasm enclosing a nucleus, and the myoblast is situated beneath the epithelial layer as in the medusæ (HERTWIGS), some hydroids (KOROTNEFF, CIAMICIAN), and a number of polyps (HERTWIGS, JOURDAN). It is, however, possible that some of the epithelio-muscular cells may retain this form permanently.

III.

DEVELOPMENT OF THE COLONY.

The primary polyp of *Renilla*, produced by sexual reproduction from the egg, begins at a very early age to produce secondary polyps by budding, and thus builds up a community or colony of individuals organically united together. Although this process is a very common one among the Anthozoa, and is all but universal among the Alcyonaria, it possesses a special interest in the case of *Renilla*, on account of the very early period of life at which the power of asexual reproduction is developed, and more especially from the remarkably definite and constant structural relations existing between the members of the community.

§ 14. *Development and functions of the first pair of sexual polyps.*

When the larva is no more than seventy-two hours old, and is still actively swimming through the water, a pair of buds make their appearance on the dorsal side, just above the point where the dorsal and dorso-lateral septa join each other and the peduncular septum. This position of the buds is entirely constant, and I have never seen the least variation from it in the many hundreds of specimens examined.

The buds, as shown at p^1. in figs. 103, 104, appear as slight rounded elevations, with darker centres and without visible septa or mouth-openings. Upon making a longitudinal section through the bud at this stage (*i.e.*, a section transverse to the axial polyp) we find that the darker centre is produced by an ingrowth of ectoderm (fig. 173, *st.*) which forms the first rudiment of the œsophagus, and is therefore a stomodæum. The lamella (*sl.*) is pushed inwards for some distance so as to form a kind of pouch, filled with a solid mass of ectoderm. The lamella at the bottom of the stomodæum then becomes perforated, so that the ectoderm becomes continuous with the entoderm, though there is still no cavity in the œsophagus. The process is fundamentally like the formation of the stomodæum in the axial polyp, but the mouth-opening is differently formed. The cavity of the œsophagus appears as a funnel-shaped depression at the inner end of the stomodæum opening within into the gastric cavity of the axial polyp and terminating outwardly in the solid plug of ectodermic tissue which forms the stomodæum. The cells of this plug are small and rounded, without definite arrangement. Farther inwards the ectoderm cells assume an irregularly columnar arrangement on either side of the cavity, and at the inner end of the stomodæum become definitely columnar and graduate insensibly into the entoderm cells around the lips of the œsophagus.

The cavity of the œsophagus soon breaks through to the exterior, forming a small oval opening, the mouth, which gradually becomes elongated in the dorso-ventral plane until it has the form of a long cleft. The cells of the stomodæum become at the same time of a high columnar form, and cilia make their appearance at the inner ends of those on the ventral side. By the action of these cilia strong currents are drawn into the colony through the mouths of the buds which are held widely open. These currents may be readily shown by adding finely-powdered carmine to the water, when the particles may be seen to be sucked with force into the mouths of the buds. In this manner large quantities of water are sucked into the cavity of the axial polyp, whose body may thus become greatly distended. When a sufficient amount of water has been taken in, the mouths of the buds are tightly closed, and the water is thus retained. The water thus taken in is kept in active circulation by means of the cilia which cover the entoderm. The currents, which are rendered plainly visible by the particles suspended in the fluid, follow a definite course. In the upper chamber of the peduncle the current sets always backwards, and the fluid flows thence into the lower chamber through the openings along the sides, and at the posterior end of the peduncular septum. In the lower chamber the current flows forwards into the anterior part of the gastric cavity.

It is by means of the fluid contained in the gastric cavity that the young polyp is enabled to effect the active creeping movements which it now performs. The *modus operandi* is as follows. The anterior part of the body being well distended, an active peristaltic contraction of the circular muscles takes place and the fluid is thus forced backwards into the posterior region (which may now be termed the peduncle). The latter consequently becomes much elongated, somewhat as the ambulacral "foot" of an Echinoderm is protruded, and the body is pushed forwards a short distance. The circular muscles then relax and the longitudinal ones contract in such a manner as to pull the posterior region forwards towards the anterior part which adheres to the bottom. By the constant repetition of this process the whole organism moves slowly forwards. The creeping movements are very irregular, since the action of the muscles is not uniform. The longitudinal muscles frequently contract more on one side than on the other, so that the body sways and twists about from side to side, often turning completely over and undergoing all kinds of contortions. Nevertheless the organism often creeps for a considerable distance and may even crawl up the perpendicular sides of a glass vessel. The same power of active movement is possessed by the adult colony, and the conditions under which the organism lives are obviously such as to render this power of vital importance to the creature. Living as it does on shifting beds of sand, the colony would be buried and smothered were it not for this power of creeping. If, however, a *Renilla* colony be covered with sand in the aquarium, it soon works its way to the surface and the polyps are enabled to expand in the water.

In the vital necessity of the power of movement lies no doubt the explanation of the very early appearance of the buds. If the young polyp, upon abandoning its free-swimming life and settling in the sand, possessed no means of taking in water and thus of creeping, it would be very apt to be smothered in the shifting sand. By the very early appearance of the buds the young polyp is enabled to imbibe water and to creep as soon as the sedentary life is assumed, and is thereby preserved from destruction.

This view receives a strong confirmation upon comparing *Leptogorgia* with *Renilla* in this respect. The former does not possess the power of creeping but attaches itself at an early age to solid objects in situations where it is not likely to be buried. Precisely as we should expect under the foregoing view, the buds of *Leptogorgia* do not appear at an early period. In my specimens, in fact, they had not made their appearance at the end of nearly two months (!), whereas in *Renilla* they appear at the end of three days.

As the buds become older and more fully developed they gradually cease to perform the function of imbibing water. It is however assumed by younger buds and is in turn lost by the latter as they become older. Throughout the entire life of the organism this function is performed by the sexual polyps in their early stages. The function is lost, so far as I have observed, as the bud becomes mature and is adapted to perform the functions of nutrition and reproduction. This may readily be demonstrated by placing a contracted colony in a vessel of water containing finely divided carmine. The water is forcibly sucked in through the mouths of all of the young marginal buds, but never through the adult polyps. This function is performed by the zooids during their entire existence ; so that the latter structures are physio-logically identical with the young sexual polyps (see § 21).

As may be seen in fig. 173, the bud lies at first almost entirely inside the primary polyp, projecting inwards from the body wall and forming only a very slight prominence on the exterior. As development proceeds the bud is pushed outwards so as to form an obtusely conical elevation on the exterior (fig. 178, p^1.). At the same time the entoderm grows downwards from the tip of the bud in eight radiating plates (fig.

178ᵉ) stretching between the wall of the œsophagus and the lateral wall of the bud. These are the septa. They have the same structure as in the young primary polyp, consisting of two layers of entoderm cells separated by a delicate supporting lamella which joins that of the body-wall. As the septa are formed the outer wall of the bud becomes divided into eight lobes (fig. 184ᵃ) which correspond with the eight chambers of the body. As the bud grows outwards (cf. fig. 205,) the septa grows inwards (i.e., downwards toward the axial polyp) so that their lower extremities remain at about the level of the body-wall of the primary polyp.

The septa when first formed stand at nearly equal intervals from each other, though those on the dorsal side are often a little more crowded than the others. As the bud develops further the septa assume a definite arrangement as shown in fig. 184ᵃ. The ventral pair approach more closely so that the ventral chamber, which is opposite one end of the elongated mouth, becomes distinctly narrower than the two adjoining ventro-lateral chambers. As shown by the later development, the narrow ventral chamber is homologous with the ventral chamber of the axial polyp and we are thus enabled to determine the orientation of the young polyp. We find that the dorso-ventral axis of the bud has a constant position with reference to the primary polyp, which is shown in fig. 184ᵃ; a–p represents the long axis of the primary polyp, and d–v the dorso-ventral axis of the bud. The latter cuts the former nearly at a right angle, but is always inclined slightly forwards (a represents the anterior extremity of the axial polyp).

——————

I will add a brief account of the habits of the young colony at this stage.

If the creature be left to itself it gradually comes to a state of rest, burying the peduncle in the sand. The body always assumes nearly the same position, the dorsal side (as determined by the interior structure) being held upwards and the buds extending horizontally on either side. The anterior part of the main polyp, with its crown of tentacles, is directed obliquely upwards and forwards. This position is maintained throughout all the following stages, and this is, I believe, a fact of the greatest importance which stands in causal connexion with the bilateral symmetry of the organism.

The tentacles of the axial polyp may at this stage be entirely retracted into the anterior part of the body. This is effected by the invagination of the oral end of the body, the tentacles being at the same time strongly contracted. When fully expanded they are held nearly horizontally with the outer portion curving gently backwards. When the polyp is hungry the tentacles are moved actively back and forth, somewhat after the fashion of a Synapta, but without regularity. If supplied with food, such as Gasteropod veligers, the tentacles close eagerly upon it, and it is held for some time closely clasped by them. They are then taken into the œsophagus and passed in a bolus down to its lower portion where they remain for some time, the lower opening of the œsophagus remaining tightly closed. The bolus is at length suddenly passed into the stomach and retained during digestion in its upper portion. I was unable to discover any indication of intra-cellular digestion. The contents of the veliger shells were dissolved out and were then circulated through the gastric cavity in the form of oil globules. The empty shells were finally ejected through the œsophagus by a reversed peristaltic action.

In *Leptogorgia*, which was fed with oyster larvæ, the process was slightly different. The larvæ were passed into the œsophagus until a large bolus was accumulated at the lower end. The bolus was then passed into the stomach and closely clasped by the short mesenterial filaments. It was thus held for two or three hours, and its remains were finally ejected through the mouth. This seems to indicate that the filaments are intimately concerned in the process of digestion; but, as before, I could not determine the mode of action of the cells.

This observation is interesting, taken in connexion with KRUKENBERG's physiological studies upon the nature of the filaments in the Actiniæ.[*] From experiments on artificial digestion he is led to conclude that the mesenterial filaments are mainly or entirely concerned in the act of digestion—so far, at least, as proteid matters are concerned—and my observations seem to point in the same direction.

§ 15. *Arrangement and succession of the sexual polyps.*

I have not succeeded in raising the young colonies in the aquarium beyond the stage shown in fig. 178, and my observations on the later stages were made from specimens procured in the sand, which were found in every stage of development. Hence I cannot give the rate of development, since the young colonies develop very slowly or not at all when kept in aquaria. Large numbers of them were examined and the succession of the buds was found to be nearly constant in early stages though somewhat variable in later ones.

The buds develop always symmetrically in pairs with wonderful regularity, as the accompanying series of figures will show. The appearance of the first pair has already been described.

The second pair invariably appear just behind the first (fig. 182, p^2.), and their mode of development is quite like that of the first pair. As soon as the dorso-ventral axis can be distinguished, they are found to be placed like those of the first pair, though the obliquity is less marked, and the axis of the buds often form a right angle with the long axis of the primary polyp. The second pair are at first quite disconnected from the first pair, but soon fuse to some extent with them, the buds being separated by a thin partition wall which terminates by a free edge below (fig. 204, *e.*). The third pair are formed some time after the second, a short distance in front of and obliquely below the first. As before, they are at first quite separate from the other buds, but soon fuse with the first pair (see figs. 204 to 207). The

---

[*] Vergleichend-physiologische Studien an den Küsten der Adria, Erste Abtheilung, 1880.

fourth pair (Fig. 185, p^4.) arise in front of and slightly below the third in the same manner as the other buds.

Up to this point the order of succession is almost invariable. The sequence in the appearance of the remaining buds is subject to considerable variation, though their position is definite and constant. They make their appearance in the angles between the buds already formed, and in the angles between these and the primary polyp; this will be rendered clear by an inspection of figs. 186 to 188.

In fig. 185 a fifth pair (p^5.) have appeared between the first and second. In fig. 186 two additional pairs (p^6. and p^7.) have appeared; one pair (p^6.) are placed in the posterior angles between p^2. and the primary polyp, and the other (p^7.) are between p^1. and p^3.

Fig. 187 is a still older colony in which five new pairs, besides the seven of fig. 186, have appeared.

Of these new pairs p^{12}. are placed in front of the entire series, while the remaining four (p^{11}., p^{10}., p^9., and p^8.) are placed in the angles between p^3.–p^4., p^1.–p^5, p^3.–p^2., and p^2.–p^6., respectively.

Fig. 188 is a still later stage with the tentacles retracted.

The buds are designated as before. Only one additional pair has appeared (p^{13}.), but those of the last stage have greatly increased in size, as may be seen by comparing the corresponding buds marked p^{10}. in the two figures.

The colony has now assumed the form of a flattened disc, with polyps in various stages of growth situated all around the edge. This form results from the circumstance that the secondary polyps grow out laterally away from the primary polyps, and the younger polyps borne in their angles are thus carried further and further away from the centre of the group. The longitudinal axes of the secondary polyps radiate in every direction from the central point. The posterior part of the axial polyp (ped.) may now be recognised as the peduncle of the colony.

It has already been noted that the third bud lies a little below the level of the first, and the fourth a little below the third. The buds are therefore arranged on each side in an oblique line, extending forwards and downwards. This line is continued by succeeding buds so that the anterior buds finally come to lie partly on the lower side of the axial polyp, as at p^{12}. in fig. 188. The two lines of buds finally meet one another at the ventral side of the axial polyp. The latter meanwhile bends gradually upwards so that the two lines of buds are kept nearly horizontal, and when they meet are situated at the anterior edge of the disc, and not at its lower side. The axial polyp is thus cut off entirely from the edge, and now rises from the upper side of the disc. This process will be rendered clear by an inspection of fig. 189, where $ax.$ designates the axial polyp, and p^{12}., p^{12}., the foremost pair of lateral buds which have united behind the axial polyp at the point x. In the angle between p^{12}., p^{12}. has appeared a median bud which completes the outline of the disc in front.

The portion of the axial cell which is included in the disc, forms the "polyp-cell" and its free portion is what is usually termed the polyp. The latter may be entirely invaginated into the former by the action of the longitudinal muscles of the septa. The calyx-teeth, which have meanwhile increased greatly in length, are situated just at the upper surface of the disc, and when the polyp is retracted they radiate from the opening of the cell (see fig. 189).

The foregoing account of the enclosure of the axial polyp will apply equally well to the secondary polyps. On account of the continual appearance of young buds in the angles between older ones, each of the latter is bordered by younger polyps on each side. The latter gradually extend downwards, and finally meet behind the older polyp which at the same time bends upwards, and thus becomes enclosed within the disc. This is shown in fig. 188, where p^7. and p^{10}. are already extending behind p^1.

As mentioned at p. 789, the ventral compartment of the polyp never has a calyx-tooth, a fact which is rendered conspicuous when the polyps are retracted (see fig. 189). When the polyp turns upwards and is enclosed in the disc, the ventral chamber necessarily comes to be situated on the outer side of the polyp or away from the centre of the group.

By the union of the lateral lines of buds the outline of the disc is completed at front, and the marginal buds now form an unbroken series from one side to the other behind the axial polyp. At the posterior part of the disc, however, the outline is never completed and a permanent sinus remains in which the peduncle is attached. This is due to the cessation of the formation of lateral buds in the posterior angle after three or four buds have been formed (see fig. 189).

§ 16. Formation of organs in the secondary polyps.

The early development of the bud, including the formation of the œsophagus and septa, has already been described; but we have still to consider the development of organs in later stages. The bud agrees in the main with the primary polyp, but there are certain important differences in the sequence of development of certain organs.

a. Development of the calyx-teeth.

As the bud grows outwards the outer ends of the chambers grow out into obtusely conical projections, which ultimately form the calyx-teeth, though they are at first closely similar to tentacles. As observed by KÖLLIKER and EISEN, they are formed in definite sequence, and I can in the main confirm the accounts of these authors. This sequence cannot be observed in the appearance of the calyx-teeth of the primary polyp, and is only obscurely shown in the buds which are first formed. As the colony increases in size, however, the sequence becomes very marked, especially in the posterior parts of the disc where the calyx-teeth are usually longer than elsewhere.

Figs. 190 to 193 illustrate the most usual succession of the teeth. The first to develop are those of the ventro-lateral chambers (fig. 190). These are often enormously elongated, especially in the posterior parts of the disc, and they remain for a long time distinctly longer than the others, as may be seen in fig. 193. After a considerable interval they are followed by the calyx-tooth of the dorsal chamber (fig. 191). The lateral teeth appear nearly simultaneously; but so far as I have observed, the median-lateral teeth usually precede somewhat the dorso-lateral. This is sometimes quite decided (fig. 192); but in a few cases the dorso-lateral teeth are first to appear. According to KÖLLIKER this is the rule, and he states that when five teeth are present, the missing teeth are always those of the median-lateral chambers. The ventral chamber very rarely develops a tooth. In younger buds, when all of the teeth are formed, they usually increase pretty regularly in length from above downwards, and this gradation is more marked usually in posterior parts of the disc. In later stages, the difference gradually becomes less, until the teeth are of nearly equal length. In the rare cases of the appearance of a ventral tooth this is always smaller than the others. The calyx-teeth vary greatly in length in different colonies. We note, finally, that the calyx-teeth are usually all formed before the tentacles appear, whereas the reverse is true of the primary polyp.

It is surprising to find this regular succession in the appearance of the calyx-teeth, which must be structures much younger, phylogenetically, than the tentacles. It may perhaps depend upon the circumstance that the polyps are in early stages placed side by side, so that the upper and lower calyx-teeth are more directly exposed to the environment. This does not, however, account for the absence of a tooth on the ventral chamber, and in our ignorance of the functions of the teeth in early stages, it is useless to speculate on the matter. In the mature bud the teeth probably serve as an armature for the mouths of the polyp-cells, since they are then stiffened with spicules and must form an effective defence. They can hardly perform such an office, however, in the young buds and in the zooids, though their early and ample development in both these cases indicates that they must perform some function. The very brilliant and beautiful phosphorescence of the colony appears to have its principal seat in the calyx-teeth of the young buds; but this can hardly throw any light upon their function.

Whatever be their function, the sequence in the development of the calyx-teeth seems to stand in no relation with the definite succession of the tentacles in some Zoantharia, but is dependent upon some special unknown conditions peculiar to the *Renilla* colony.

b. Development of the tentacles.

The formation of the tentacles agrees entirely with that of the tentacles of the primary polyp, and calls for no special remark. They make their appearance simultaneously, after the formation of the calyx-teeth, as conical outgrowths of the compartments between the mouth and the calyx-teeth. They are at first simple, but soon become pinnate, the pinnæ developing somewhat irregularly in pairs at the bases of the tentacles.

c. Development of the mesenterial filaments.

The mesenterial filaments are formed in essentially the same manner as in the primary polyp, appearing as thickenings on the edges of the septa. They differ however in one striking feature from the filaments of the primary polyp, viz.: in the order of their appearance. The dorsal filaments in the latter are last to appear and slowest in development, whereas in the buds they are in many cases first to appear, and in all cases develop at first more rapidly than the other six. This agrees entirely with KÖLLIKER's observations on the development of the secondary polyps in *Halisceptrum* ('Pennatuliden,' p. 161) in which the dorsal filaments are well formed before a trace of the other six can be made out.

This remarkable contrast between the development of the filaments of the primary and secondary polyps shows clearly that in searching for the relations between the various groups of polyps, as indicated by their embryology, we are not justified in comparing the egg-development of one form with the bud-development of another, or in taking the structure of the bud as any necessary indication of the succession of the parts in the egg-embryo. That the importance of this principle has been unconsciously disregarded will, I think, be clear from the following citations.

MOSELEY writes in his admirable paper on *Heliopora* and *Sarcophyton* (Phil. Trans. Vol. 166, 1876, p. 121): "It seems extremely difficult to reconcile the extraordinary succession of the mesenteries in the development of the Zoantharians, discovered by LACAZE-DUTHIERS, with the facts presented by Alcyonarians. Did the development of the eight mesenteries of Alcyonaria correspond with that of the first eight mesenteries formed in Actiniadæ, the first mesenteries formed would be either the lateral dorsal or lateral ventral; but these are those which are most rudimentary in the zooids of *Sarcophyton*. Moreover the mesenterial filaments of the two lateral pairs of septa are in the development of Actiniadæ the first to appear, and not the dorsal, which are longest in the Alcyonarian polyps and most persistent in the zooids. Apparently, however, development in Alcyonarians follows a different course."

These words seem clearly to imply that the greater length of the dorsal filaments and their persistence in the zooids indicates their earlier development in the embryo.

KÖLLIKER states explicitly ('Pennatuliden,' p. 427): "Die Septa und Septula sind Falten des Entoderm und entstehen wahrscheinlich alle zugleich (ich), dagegen bilden sich in erster Linie nur an zweien derselben Verdickungen des Entoderma (Mesenterial-filamente) und später erst treten solche auch an den andern 6 Septa gleichzeitig auf." At p. 434, he even extends this statement so as to apply to the entire group of Alcyonaria: "Bei den Alcyonarien treten nun allerdings auch *zwei* Mesenterial-filamente früher als die anderen auf, allein diese stehen *dicht beisammen*, und bilden sich nach allem, was wir wissen, alle acht Septa auf einmal."

Nevertheless, in *Renilla* at least, the exact reverse of what is indicated by the passages cited is actually the case; and the presumption is that the same holds true in *Sarcophyton*, *Halisceptrum* and other Alcyonaria.

The facts presented by the bud-development of *Renilla* tend to show that a definite sequence in the appearance of symmetrically repeated parts may very readily be acquired or modified through the action of secondary causes which are, however, for the most part too obscure to be recognised.

§ 17. *Development of the zooids.*

a. The exhalent zooid.

The exhalent zooid (*ex.* in all the figures) makes its appearance some time after the appearance of the first pair of secondary polyps and always before the second pair are developed. It occupies always the same position, viz. : on the median line of the dorsal compartment a short distance in front of the pair of buds (fig. 181). Its early development is in all respects identical with that of the sexual polyps, and when the septa are well established they are found to have the same arrangement as in the latter. The ventral chamber is very narrow and remains always without a calyx tooth. As the zooid increases in size a short calyx-tooth appears on each of the other chambers, and these are developed simultaneously so far as observed (figs. 188, 189). The zooid is in this stage closely similar to the mouth of the cell of a sexual polyp when the latter is contracted (*cf.* fig. 189). The zooid remains in essentially the same condition during its whole existence, but the calyx-teeth become much more elongated and the ventral chamber becomes so small as almost to disappear. No tentacles are ever developed and I have never observed the least rudiment of them.

We find that the dorso-ventral axis of the zooid, which may at once be determined by the elongation of the mouth and the position of the ventral compartment, coincides with the long axis of the primary polyp; and furthermore that the ventral side is turned towards the posterior part of the latter. This relation of the axis is constant, though the axis of the zooid sometimes forms a small angle with the long axis of axial polyp. It sometimes happens that two exhalent zooids are formed. In this case one of them is usually placed in the normal position and the other lies at one side with its axis more or less oblique. In one case the zooid was devoid of a mouth-opening.

b. The inhalent zooids.

An especial interest attaches to the development of these zooids on account of the curious and constant relations existing between their axis and between these and the axis of the sexual polyps.

The zooid develops in quite the same manner as the young sexual polyp or the exhalent zooid, but never progresses beyond the stage in which two calyx-teeth (those of the ventro-lateral chambers) are formed. The zooid is therefore structurally as well as physiologically (see p. 784) identical with the young sexual polyp. In the fully-developed zooid the œsophagus is of an oval form, elongated slightly in the dorso-ventral axis, and connecting with the exterior through an oval mouth. The inner wall of the œsophagus is covered on its ventral side with powerful cilia, by the action of which water may be drawn in from the exterior in precisely the same manner as by the young sexual polyps. The mouth is furnished with a sphincter muscle by which it may be tightly closed when the cavities of the colony are sufficiently distended with water. As already described, the sexual buds, as they increase in size, gradually cease to perform the function of drawing in water. The zooids, however, retain this function permanently and have been specialised for this purpose alone since they have neither tentacles, mesenterial filaments, nor reproductive organs. The sexual buds hand over their early function, as it were, to the zooids as they become themselves adapted to play another part in the economy of the organism.

As shown in fig. 202 the two calyx-teeth of the zooids become greatly elongated and in some specimens, especially in the posterior parts of the disc, may attain an enormous development. Their walls are soft and flexible and are considerably thickened towards the tips where the cells assume a columnar form. It seems very probable that they may perform tactile functions, but I have been unable to demonstrate this in living specimens.

The chambers have the usual arrangement, there being always a somewhat narrow ventral chamber enclosed between two wide ventro-lateral ones. The five upper chambers are always smaller than the ventro-lateral ones and are nearly equal in size. It is therefore always easy to distinguish the dorso-ventral axis of the zooid, which for the sake of brevity I shall call simply the *axis*.

The zooids are produced in pairs like the sexual polyps, though with less regularity. The first pair (fig. 185, z^1.) make their appearance on the dorsal side of the axial polyp near the bases of the first pair of sexual polyps, at the time when four or five pairs of sexual polyps have appeared. Behind these there appear two or three pairs of zooids somewhat irregularly placed on the upper side of the axial polyp. They are arranged (cf. figs. 188, 189) on either side of a longitudinal space which remains permanently free from zooids and is very conspicuous in the fully-formed colony. KÖLLIKER has termed this area the *keel* (Kiel), and it is of common occurrence among the Pennatulida. In the adult colony it extends forwards from the posterior sinus about half-way across the disc. The exhalent zooid is placed at its anterior end and groups of inhalent zooids border it on either side. The axes of these zooids are very irregularly placed, but as a rule the ventral side of the zooid is turned towards the posterior part of the colony.

The remaining zooids appear on the dorsal side and in the median line of the sexual polyp-cells, and a constant relation exists between the axis of the zooids and of the polyps on which they are placed. For the sake of convenience I shall term these zooids *dorsal zooids* to distinguish them from the *marginal zooids* which border the keel.

Four dorsal zooids, to begin with, make their appearance on the upper side of each polyp-cell. They are formed successively, proceeding from the base of the polyp outwards towards the oral extremity, as may be seen upon comparison of figs. 187, 188, 189. In fig. 187 the polyp p^5. has a single dorsal zooid, and p^2. has two. In fig. 189 the polyp p^3. has three zooids and p^7. has four.

The bilateral arrangement of the zooids is well shown by fig. 187, in which the positions of the zooids are accurately represented. With two exceptions each zooid has its counterpart on the opposite half of the colony. The exceptions are the marginal zooid $zm.$, and the dorsal zooid $zd.$, which appear on the right side only.

The zooids are sometimes formed on very young sexual buds, as at p^4. in fig. 187. This recalls the very early appearance of the power of budding in the axial polyp. Upon examining the axis of a dorsal zooid we find that in many cases it coincides with the long axis of the sexual polyp on which it is seated, and where it does not the axis of the zooid forms less than a right angle with that of the polyp. Moreover, the ventral chamber of the zooid is always placed at that end of the axis which is turned towards the basal part of the polyp and therefore towards the centre of the colony. There is a strong tendency in the zooid to assume a position on the secondary polyp corresponding with the position of the exhalent zooid with respect to the primary polyp (see p. 791); and the variations from this position caused by the greater or less obliquity of the axis must be considered as departures from the type. Upon the axial polyp only one zooid as a rule, though sometimes two, appears in front of the exhalent zooid.

Multiplication of the zooids.

The zooids have thus far been described as if remaining simple, as is really the case up to the stage shown in fig. 188. Soon after this, however, the zooids themselves become centres of multiplication and each zooid becomes the parent of a whole group of secondary zooids. It is therefore necessary to distinguish primary and secondary zooids as we have recognised primary and secondary sexual polyps.

The axis of the primary dorsal zooid, as we have seen, stands in a definite relation to that of the sexual polyp. The axes of the secondary zooid, on the contrary, show no direct relation to those of the sexual polyp but *to those of the primary zooid.* Hence we must regard the latter as the real parent of the secondary zooids, though these appear to arise as buds on the dorsal side of the polyp-cell and not directly upon the primary zooid. We must, at any rate, grant that the primary zooid is a centre of force which controls the development of the secondary zooids, and it will be convenient for our purpose to consider the latter as the progeny of the former.

The multiplication of the zooids varies exceedingly, as we might expect from their rudimentary structure and great numbers, but the variation affects only the number and arrangement of the zooids, leaving the relations between their axes unaltered. Figs. 194 to 203 illustrate the multiplication from a simple zooid (fig. 194) to a group of eighteen. The figures, it will be understood, are not drawn from different stages of an individual group but represent a number of different groups in various stages of development.

In what may be regarded as the typical case a group of four zooids is first formed (fig. 199). The upper one (d.), situated at the dorsal side of the primary zooid (p.), is usually first to appear (figs. 195-197,) but the lateral zooids (l.l'.) may appear, singly or together, before the upper one (see fig. 198). In the group of four the primary zooid is distinguished by its greater size and by the possession of calyx-teeth on the ventro-lateral chambers. The ventral chambers of the zooids (v.) are turned away from the centre of the group. Thus the axes of the lateral zooids form an angle of 90° with that of the primary zooid, and the axis of the upper zooid is 180° from that of the primary zooid.

New zooids now make their appearance in irregular succession in the angle between the four already formed (figs. 200-202) so that the group then consists typically of eight zooids. The same relation of the axes holds good for the new zooids —i.e., the ventral chamber is turned outwards, or away from the centre of the group. The superiority in size of the primary zooid is still marked and its calyx-teeth are very well developed. In most, though not in all, cases the upper zooid also acquires a pair of calyx-teeth as shown in the figures, and sometimes one of the lateral zooids also (fig. 202, l.). Most of the secondary zooids remain however without calyx-teeth, though the ventro-lateral chambers are always larger than the others. The ventral chamber is always very narrow in the zooids which have calyx-teeth, but in the other zooids it is often scarcely narrower than the ventro-lateral chambers. The axis of the zooid can however be always recognised by the elongation of the mouth and the crowding of the six upper septa.

Many of the subsequently formed zooids develop in the same manner as those already described, appearing in the angles between pre-existing zooids and having their ventral chambers turned away from the centre of the entire group. In some cases, however, the secondary zooids become in their turn centres of multiplication, thus forming minor groups which repeat, more or less completely, the formation of the primary group. This is shown in fig. 203. The primary zooid of the system is marked p., and above it lies the dorsal secondary zooid (d.) corresponding with the upper zooid in fig. 199. A considerable number of the lateral zooids are simple and their axes are related to that of the primary zooid (as may be seen from the position of their ventral chambers v.v.). At x., however, is a group of four zooids which are arranged about a centre of their own and form a secondary group quite similar to the primary group shown in fig. 199. The principal zooid (p^{11}.) of this secondary group has the usual position with respect to the primary group and appears to correspond with the zooid x. of fig. 202.   The three other zooids are evidently placed with reference to p^{11}. and not to p^1.   Thus the zooid d''. has its ventral chamber turned *towards* the centre of the main group and *away from* that of the secondary group.   Hence d''. is the offspring of p^{11}. and the grandchild of p^1.

There appear to be in fig. 203 two other secondary centres, but each is represented by two or three zooids only.   Thus a, b, and c seem to be arranged about the centre y, while d', e, and perhaps f, are arranged about a centre at z.   It is rare to find the secondary groups completely or symmetrically formed, and in many, perhaps most, cases no secondary centres can be certainly identified.   In fact, I have seen only two cases in which the secondary groups were as perfectly formed as at x. in fig. 203.

Review.

The close correspondence between the mode of budding of the zooids and of the sexual polyps must already have struck the attention of the reader.   If the group of four zooids shown in fig. 199 be compared with the group consisting of three sexual polyps and the exhalent zooid (fig. 181) the composition of the two groups is found to be the same.   If the axial polyp in fig. 181 be turned upwards at its anterior part, as actually happens at a later stage, it will have the same relation to the exhalent zooid as that existing between the lower and upper zooids of fig. 199, and the two lateral buds in fig. 181 when turned upwards have precisely the same position as the lateral zooids in fig. 199.

Similarly, we may compare the group of eight zooids (fig. 202) with the groups of eight shown in figs. 184, 205 and 206 (these are seen from the ventral side so that the dorsal member of the group, the exhalent zooid, does not show directly).   It is scarcely necessary to remind the reader that I do not mean that the corresponding members of the two groups are homologous with each other, but only that they have been produced by a similar form of asexual multiplication.

Summing up these results, we find that the multiplication of the zooids conforms to a definite law, which upon comparison is found to be identical with that which rules the budding of the sexual polyps.

§ 18. *Closure of the peduncular canals.*

We have finally to describe the manner in which the two canals of the peduncle become closed in front and thus complete the canal-system.   As described in the introduction, these canals are in the adult completely closed in front, whereas in the young they communicate freely with the gastric cavity of the axial polyp.

a. The dorsal canal.

The closure of the dorsal canal is effected by the free edge of the peduncular septum growing forwards and finally uniting with the dorsal wall just anterior to the exhalent zooid. This is illustrated by figs. 204 to 207. In fig. 204 the free edge (e.) is still some distance behind the zooid (ex.). In the next figure it has advanced further forwards and in fig. 207 has nearly passed the zooid. The edge finally unites with the dorsal wall at about the stage of fig. 187 and the canal is completely closed. These stages in the forward movement of the edge of the septum are shown also in dorsal view in figs. 181, 186 and 185.

As the septum travels forwards its edge stretches between the bases of the dorsal pair of septa and the latter gradually extend down upon the lower side of the peduncular septum in a manner which it is difficult to describe, and is scarcely shown in the figures. In fig. 181 the edge may be seen stretching between the dorsal septa far behind the dorsal mesenterial filaments (d.f.). In fig. 205 the edge of the septum and the filaments have nearly met. In fig. 206 the lower ends of the dorsal filaments lie below the peduncular septum, and in fig. 207, finally, the filaments and septa lie for more than half their length on the lower side of the peduncular septum.

b. The ventral canal.

The closure of this canal is effected by an entirely different process which I have not been able to follow out completely. It has already been mentioned (p. 786) that the partition between the first two sexual buds on each side ends below by a free edge (fig. 204). From this point a delicate flap or fold of membrane extends for a short distance inwards on the under side of the peduncular septum (fig. 204, fl.). The latter bends rather suddenly upwards at this level to terminate by the free edge (e). in front. In a later stage these flaps extend still further inwards so as nearly to meet on the under side of the septum. The edge of the flap also extends obliquely upwards and forwards across the base of the bud (fig. 205). Still later the two flaps unite below the peduncular septum and form a single membrane extending entirely across the upper part of the ventral canal and ending by a smooth round edge below (fig. 206). At the sides the membrane is slung to the body-wall by fibrous strands like those which suspend the peduncular septum (see p. 768), and it now extends nearly across the base of the bud.

In the latest stage observed (fig. 207) the membrane extends at the sides nearly around the body and has united with delicate irregular outgrowths from the ventral and ventro-lateral septa. Thus the ventral canal is separated by an incomplete partition from the anterior part of the axial polyp where the septa, mesenterial filaments and other organs are situated. There is still, however, a very large rounded opening in the middle of the partition through which the currents of the gastric fluid still flow. In later stages this opening closes up completely, probably by the approximation and union of the edges of the membrane, but I have been unable to follow this since the walls of the body become very opaque through the appearance of great numbers of spicules.

In the adult the peduncular septum appears to be split horizontally in front into two layers between which lies the cavity of the axial polyp. The development of the parts shows that this is not really the case. The upper layer alone is a direct continuation of the septum, while the lower layer is a secondary formation produced by outgrowths from the walls of the body and the septa.

The specimen represented in fig. 207 shows an interesting abnormal condition of the tentacles which deserves mention. When first discovered the two lower lateral tentacles on the left side of the axial polyp were aborted, possessing only a single pair of rudimentary pinnæ. *The two corresponding tentacles of the first lateral bud on the same side were aborted in a precisely similar manner* (see the figure). The specimen was kept alive for a fortnight, but unfortunately died before the other buds had acquired their tentacles. Meanwhile the aborted tentacles grew to about half the size of the normal ones.

The rudimentary condition of the two corresponding tentacles in the primary and secondary polyps may have been due to accidental mutilation, but the chances against such a coincidence seem very great. If on the other hand it were due to the inheritance by the bud of a mutilation or monstrosity in the parent the case would be very interesting.

IV.

GENERAL CONSIDERATIONS.

§ 19. *The systematic relations of* Renilla.

In reviewing the development of the *Renilla* colony, we are naturally led to inquire whether the arrangement and succession of the buds throws any light on the relations of *Renilla* to other members of the Pennatulacea. Here, as in the case of the homologies of the organs of the individual, the basis for comparison is very narrow on account of the imperfect state of our knowledge. Fortunately, however, the evidence is enough to show how the mode of budding in *Renilla* may readily be reduced to the ordinary type as exhibited in the penniform Pennatulids, as for instance in *Pennatula* or *Pteroides*.

KÖLLIKER was so fortunate as to obtain a very young colony of *Pteroides Lacazii* (KÖLL.), a representative of the typical Penniformes, and his valuable and interesting observations, when compared with my own on *Renilla*, are enough to show that the mode of growth is essentially the same in these widely different forms. In *Pteroides* ('Pennatuliden,' p. 356, plate xxiii., figs. 214, 215) as in *Renilla* there is a primary or axial polyp which produces paired lateral buds; the order of their appearance was not determined nor was it ascertained whether new buds are interpolated between older ones. The young colonies of *Renilla* and *Pteroides* are in this stage essentially alike, as may be seen on comparison of Kölliker's fig. 214 (*Pteroides*) with my figs. 186 or 187. In both, the axial polyp terminates in the median line in front and the structure of the colony is strictly bilateral.

The subsequent history of the axial polyp was not followed nor has this ever actually been done save in *Umbellularia*,* which is an exceedingly aberrant form, and may for the present be left out of consideration. Inferring its history, however, from a study of the adult forms, Kölliker makes the following general statement (*l.c.*, p. 420) : "Die typische Bau dieser Stöcke ist ohne Kenntniss ihrer Entwicklung nicht zu verstehen, und bemerke ich daher vor Allem, das der erste aus dem Embryo hervorgehende Polyp, den ich den Haupt, oder axial Polypen nenne, wahrscheinlich nicht überall in derselben Weise sich verhält. Bei den Einen Formen, wie bei den *Veretilliden*, scheint derselbe sich zu erhalten und später, wie die secundär aus ihm entstandenen Individuen, einfach als Geschlectsthier zu wirken. Bei andern Abtheilungen dagegen, wie bei den *Pennatuleen*, und *Renillaceen*, verkümmert der axial *Polyp schon früh* und stellt gewissermassen *ein rein* vegetatives Individuum dar, dessen Function erlischt, sobald eine gewisse Zahl secondäre Einzelthiere gebildet sind. Sei dem wie ihm wolle, so bilden sich auf jeden Fall die späteren Einzelthiere *als seitliche Knospen* au dem ersten Polypen und beruht auf einer fortgesetzten solchen Knospenbildung wesentlich die Entstehung der ganzen Colonie."

This statement must be slightly modified, so far as the Renillaceæ are concerned ; for the axial polyp does not in this case abort but remains, as in the *Veretillidæ*, as a sexual-feeding polyp (Kölliker's statement is evidently made under the assumption that the exhalent zooid—"*Hauptzooid* "—is the aborted axial polyp, a view which has been shown to be erroneous).

Furthermore it is not certain that the axial polyp, even in the elongated *Penniformes* and *Virgulariea*, remains at the anterior end, increasing in length throughout the growth of the colony ; for Willimöes-Suhm observed (*l.c.*) that in *Umbellularia* the axial polyp does not retain its original position in the median plane, but becomes bent to one side so as to assume a lateral position, its former place being taken by one of the secondary lateral buds. Still, the evidence seems to be upon the whole in favour of the view that the primary polyp, whether remaining functionally active or becoming aborted, does retain its median position in the elongated Pennatulids and forms the central axis of the community.

In the simple elongated Pennatulids—as in the *Bathyptilea* of Kölliker—the axial polyp produces a series of simple lateral buds on each side, which have a bilaterally symmetrical arrangement, and remain simple throughout the life of the organism. From this condition, as Kölliker fully shows, a nearly complete series may be formed on the one hand through the *Protoptilea*, *Funiculinea*, *Virgularinæ* to the typical *Penniformes*, and on the other hand through the *Kophobelemnonieæ* to the *Veretillidæ*.

* Willemöes-Suhm, Ann. and Mag. of Nat. Hist., vol. xv., 1875

Upon comparison we find that the colonies of *Pteroides* and *Renilla*, though widely different in their adult state from each other and from the *Bathyptilea*, pass through a stage of development which precisely corresponds with the permanent condition of the latter group. Obviously this fact tells strongly in favour of the derivation of both the *Penniformes* and the *Renillacea* from the *Bathyptilea* or a representative group, and this is the conclusion which upon the whole appears to me most probable. So far as the *Penniformes* are concerned this conclusion is simply a reiteration of KÖL-LIKER'S conclusions, but in regard to the *Renillacea* it is entirely different. KÖLLIKER'S view is as follows (' Pennatuliden,' p. 450) :—

"Nur zu den *Renilliden* führt keine Brücke von den jetzt lebenden Pennatuliden aus und müssen wir zum Verständnisse derselben auf eine noch nicht beobachtete Urform, ähnlich den jugendlich von FRITZ MÜLLER beobachteten *Renillen* oder den Cornularien unter den Alcyoniden, zurückgehen, die der Kürze halber *Archiptilum* heissen mag. Dieses *Archiptilum* wäre also als ein freier einfacher Polyp nach Art der Edwardsien aber mit der innern Organisation der Alcyonarien zu denken und liesse ich an ihm schon eine solche Differenzirung annehmen, dass ein Stiel und ein Kiel zu unterscheiden wäre. Aus solchen Archiptileen oder weiteren Umbildungen derselben könnte man dann einerseits durch besondere Art der Knospenbildung die *Renilliden*, anderseits die Protoptileen und die Bathyptileen ableiten und wäre im ihnen das vereinigende Band der ganzen Ordnung gegeben. Die Abkunft der Archiptileen selbst anlangend, so werden wir naturgemäss auf die Hydroidpolypen geführt und kann es nach dem, was wir über den Bau von *Hybocodon*, *Tubularia*, und *Cormorpha* wissen, keine Schwierigkeiten machen, von denselben aus den Uebergang zu den gekammerten Anthozoen zu finden wie dies auch HAECKEL angedeutet hat. Diese Protanthozoen würden dann in weiterer Linie zu den Urtypen der verschiedenen Abtheilungen der Korallthiere und somit auch zu den Archiptileen sich entwickelt haben."

The development of the *Renilla* colony shows, however, that it is unnecessary to go back further than the *Bathyptilea*, so far at least as the mode of budding is concerned. The peculiar form of the colony is a result primarily of the circumstance that *the longitudinal growth of the axial polyp ceases at an early stage*, while the two series of lateral buds continue to extend forwards until they enclose the axial polyp; and secondarily of the fact that new lateral buds are constantly interpolated between those already formed, and that the lateral buds fuse with each other to some extent. If we imagine the axial polyp in fig. 189 to become greatly elongated, so as to separate the older buds from one another, and thus to leave room for the younger buds between them, we should have a colony similar to the *Bathyptilum*, i.e., a long central axis with a single series of lateral buds on each side.

KÖLLIKER'S view of the derivation of *Renilla* involves one serious difficulty on any monophyletic theory of descent. The original simple progenitor of the Alcyonaria cannot have possessed the *septum transversale* or the four peduncular septa of the higher Pennatulids, since these are structures peculiar to the Pennatulacea, and do not exist so far as known in the simple young of other Alcyonaria (*cf. Leptogorgia*, p. 768). It is hard to avoid the conclusion that these structures are intimately connected with the formation of the peculiar internal axis in those Pennatulids (including all but *Renilla*) which possess such a structure. In *Renilla reniformis* the *septum transversale* alone is developed (as the peduncular septum), but in *Renilla amethystina*, as described by KÖLLIKER and EISEN, four partitions appear in the anterior part of the peduncle (see p. 770), which appear to be homologous with the four peduncular septa by which the axis is suspended in the axis-bearing Pennatulids. If, then, the latter forms and *Renilla* have independently arisen from the *Archiptilum*, which possesses no axis, it is impossible to account for the presence of the four peduncular septa in some species of *Renilla*. Whereas, if *Renilla* is descended from an axis-bearing form resembling *Bathyptilum* the occasional appearance of four peduncular septa presents no difficulty (compare § 9).

As KÖLLIKER has shown, the lateral pinnæ (*Blätter*) of the *Penniformes* are probably derived from simple lateral buds by the appearance of a series of dorsal buds upon the latter :—

" In der That lehren die Pennatuliden mit Blättern, dass jedes Blatt anfänglich nur aus wenigen, wahrscheinlich ursprünglich nur aus Einem Polyp besteht und dass die übrigen Individuen nach und nach an der *Dorsalseite* desselben *aus ihm hervorbilden*, was theils durch *Theilungen*, theils durch *Knospenbildungen* aus ihm geschieht" (' Pennatuliden,' p. 430).

At first thought it might seem probable that this dorsal series of buds is represented in *Renilla* by the series of dorsal zooids which always appear on the upper median line of the sexual polyps. But upon examination we find that the axes of the zooids are differently placed from those of the polyps. The ventral chambers of the former face inwards (towards the centre of the disc), whereas those of the polyps in the pinnæ of the *Penniformes* face backwards ; it seems therefore improbable that they can correspond. As we shall see in a following section, it is doubtful whether the zooids of *Renilla* are homologous with (*i.e.*, directly descended from) sexual polyps. The representatives of the dorsal polyps of the pinnæ, if present at all in *Renilla*, are rather to be sought in those lateral buds of *Renilla* which do not arise directly upon the body of the axial polyp.

Summary.

The development of the colony in *Renilla* indicates its ancestral origin from a form resembling the *Bathyptileæ* from which have also been derived along different lines of descent the *Pennatuleæ* on the one hand, and the *Kophobelemnonieæ* and *Veretillidæ* on the other. In the course of this transformation an axis has probably been lost, the only indication of it at present being the persistence of the *septum transversale* (peduncular septum) and in some species of the four peduncular septa. No decisive evidence on the latter question can be adduced until the development of the axis is made known.

§ 20. *Bilateral symmetry of* Renilla.

The very striking bilateral symmetry, both of the individual polyps and of the entire community, is constantly brought before our notice in studying the anatomy and development of *Renilla*; and it is impossible to leave the subject without considering briefly the significance and origin of this symmetrical arrangement of parts.

Reviewing the symmetry of the individual, we find that is expressed, firstly, in the existence of a dorso-ventral axis, represented by certain median unpaired parts, viz. : the elongated œsophagus and mouth, the ventral chamber devoid of a calyx-tooth, the dorsal chamber with a well-developed calyx-tooth, and the dorsal and ventral median areas of longitudinal muscles. All the remaining parts are bilaterally arranged with respect to this axis, viz. : the tentacles, calyx-teeth, septa, mesenterial filaments, reproductive organs, and the septal areas of longitudinal muscles. The tentacles have a nearly perfect radiate arrangement, but the arrangement of the other organs is, to say the least, as much bilateral as radiate. The bilaterality of the calyx-teeth is strongly expressed in their mode of development, since, with the exception of the dorsal tooth, they appear in successive pairs. The septa are arranged in pairs of different lengths, and are joined together at their lower ends in a strictly bilateral arrangement. The bilaterality of the mesenterial filaments is nearly as marked as that of the septa on account of their arrangement in pairs of different length, their structure and rate of development. The reproductive organs have a strictly paired arrangement, appearing only on the dorso-lateral and ventro-lateral septa. The longitudinal muscles of the septa finally show a marked bilateral symmetry in their arrangement, being always placed on the ventral sides of the septa.

The bilaterality of many of these parts must be of comparatively recent acquisition ; for in other and lower polyps it is less evident or entirely wanting. Traces of bilateral symmetry are found in nearly all polyps, but in most of the lower forms (Zoantharia) radial symmetry, more or less complete, predominates. In the higher forms the radiating parts assume a more definitely bilateral arrangement which is very marked in the Alcyonaria and reaches its culmination in *Renilla*.[*] Hence there can be no doubt that the bilateral structure is, in part at least, due to a rearrangement of parts which were formerly radially symmetrical. The bilateral symmetry is, as it were, built upon a basis of radial symmetry ; and traces of the latter, more or less pronounced, may accordingly be seen in the bilateral arrangement of most of the parts of *Renilla*. Thus it exists almost unmodified in the grouping of the tentacles, in the septa has partly given place to a bilateral arrangement, and in the reproductive organs is scarcely or not at all to be recognised.

* See especially HAACKE, "Blastologie der Korallen," Jena. Zeitschr., Bd. xiii., 1879, and HAECKEL, "Generelle Morphologie" and "Studien z. Gastræa-theorie," Jena. Zeitschr., Bd. viii., ix., 1874-5.

In the community produced by the asexual multiplication of the individual, the bilateral symmetry is very nearly perfect. Such departures from perfect symmetry as do exist are inconstant, and appear to be due simply to slight inequalities of growth produced by varying conditions of nutrition. In the adult colony a middle plane is clearly marked by the form of the disc, position and internal structure of the axial polyp, position of the exhalent zooid and of the "keel," and the insertion of the peduncle. On either side of this axis the polyps and zooids are disposed with great regularity. Each sexual polyp has its exact counterpart on the opposite side of the disc, the axis of the two polyps making the same angle with the long axis of the colony. The groups of zooids also correspond pretty closely on the two sides, though less perfectly than the polyps.

The budding of the colony is at first strictly bilateral with surprisingly small variation; and this is true both of the polyps and of the zooids. In later stages the polyps assume a radiating arrangement, as may be seen in figs. 187 and 189, and a radial symmetry is therefore feebly indicated in the disc. This is however due simply to the cessation of growth in the long axis—*i.e.*, the axial polyp—and stands in no relation whatever to the radial symmetry of the individual. In this case we have a slightly marked secondary radial symmetry superimposed upon a primary bilateral form; and in this respect the symmetry of the colony exactly reverses the symmetry of the individual.

It seems clear therefore that the symmetry of the colony has been acquired independently of the symmetry of the individual, and it will be advantageous to consider separately the origin of the symmetry in the two cases.

If we examine the position of the individual polyps, we observe that they are so placed as to have a bilaterally symmetrical environment *which corresponds with the bilateral arrangement of their parts*. Below, they rest upon the sand; above, they are exposed to the water; so that the dorsal and ventral sides are very differently conditioned. The lateral conditions are, however, identical, since each polyp is closely united with a similar polyp on each side. It is impossible to avoid the conclusion that the bilateral environment stands in causal connexion with the bilateral structure, and the probabilities seem strongly in favour of the view that the bilateral structure —or, at least, some of its features—is a result of the environment. This view is in harmony with the prevailing general theories of symmetry which have been especially and independently developed by HAECKEL and SPENCER; namely, in SPENCER's language, that the form of symmetry depends ultimately on the nature and distribution of the incident forces acting upon the organism. These theories are so familiar as to need no review here, and I will only refer to HAECKEL's views concerning the ancestry of the Cœlenterata as developed in the papers upon the "Gastræa theory" to which reference has been made.

According to HAECKEL's theory the Cœlenterate series has been evolved from a primitive ancestral "*Protascus*," immediately derived from the *Gastræa* by the attachment of the latter at the base and the gradual acquisition of a radiate structure as a result of the equality in all directions of the lateral conditions. This theory leaves unexplained the bilateral symmetry which appears in a greater or less degree in all polyps, and HAACKE ("Blastologie der Korallen," *l.c.*) has endeavoured to explain this as the result solely of the formation of colonies. This author holds that in solitary forms like the Actiniæ the bilateral symmetry is due to descent from colony-building species, and he believes that the paired development of the septa is thus to be explained, though in precisely what manner he is unable to say.

Without accepting in all details HAACKE's views, which are only a special application of the environment theory of HAECKEL and SPENCER, it appears to me highly probable that the nature of the environment of the individual polyps in the colony will satisfactorily explain their bilateral structure. It is, of course, impossible to explain exactly how the bilaterality of the various organs is related to the bilaterality of the environment on account of our imperfect knowledge of the functions of these organs and of the laws of growth. But we cannot admit that the perfect correspondence between structure and environment is due to mere accident, and the only alternative is to regard it as the result of adaptation in the organism.

An obvious objection to this view is that it may be putting the cart before the horse; for there may be laws of nutrition or of growth, dependent upon a bilateral structure already existing, which limit the production of buds to the sides of the axial polyp. But we have seen that the zooids—which are undeveloped buds—are produced in the dorsal sides of the polyps in *Renilla*, and KÖLLIKER has shown that in other Pennatulids the zooids may appear anywhere upon the polyps. All parts of the sexual polyps therefore possess equally the power of producing buds, and hence the circumstance that each polyp is laterally united with two other individuals depends on the general form of the colony and not upon any limitation existing in the laws of growth in the individual.

Passing now to a consideration of the symmetry of the colony, we find here the same general conditions as in the individual. The young colony, as we have seen, (p. 785) assumes a definite position as soon as it begins its sedentary life, and this position is maintained during the entire existence of the organism. In this habitual position of the colony, with the peduncle rooted in the sand and the disc expanded upon the surface, the dorsal and ventral sides are quite differently conditioned, while the sides are similarly conditioned. The conditions of nutrition within the colony being equally distributed, the rate of growth must tend to be equal upon the two sides, and any modifying agency must, so far as we can see, tend to be equal upon both. There seems to be no reason to doubt that such an equality of lateral conditions, if maintained for a long period of time, would ultimately produce as perfect a bilaterality as that of *Renilla*. It is unfortunate that so little is known of the habits of other Pennatulids in which the bilateral symmetry is less marked than in *Renilla*. It is probable that a study of these forms with reference to the relation between them and their environments would throw further light upon the influence exercised by the environment upon the mode of budding and thus upon the symmetry of the colony.

§ 21. *Polymorphism of* Renilla.

Polymorphism has been definitely recognised as existing in the Pennatulacea since the publication of KÖLLIKER's great work so often cited in the foregoing pages, but the existence of " rudimentary individuals " was observed in *Renilla* by VERRILL many years earlier.[*]

We may distinguish in *Renilla* at least four kinds of individuals, viz. : *a*, the axial polyp ; *b*, the secondary sexual polyps ; *c*, the exhalent zooid ; and *d*, the inhalent zooids. Possibly two classes of the latter should be recognised, viz. : zooids which possess a pair of calyx-teeth and those which are devoid of these structures.

The question now arises whether these various forms of individuals are to be regarded as morphologically equivalent—that is, whether all are to be considered as the direct descendants of originally similar individuals which have become modified in various directions for the physiological division of labour. There can be no doubt concerning the nature of the secondary sexual polyps, for these are identical in all essentials with the axial polyp. With the various forms of zooids, however, the case is different ; for we have here to consider whether these are the aborted and rudimentary descendants of sexual polyps or are new formations which have never had a more highly organised structure than at present. To put the question in a concrete form we may inquire : Did the zooids during their past history ever possess tentacles, mesenterial filaments, and reproductive organs which were gradually lost as the polyps became specialised for the performance of a single function only, or had the zooids, when first developed in the colony, the same imperfect polypoid structure as at present ?

The problem is the same as that presented by the Siphonophora, and in the latter case has given rise to the two totally different views with which everyone is familiar. On the one hand LEUCKART, VOGT, HAECKEL, CLAUS, and others regard the various parts of the Siphonophora (*Nectocalyces, Polypites, Hydrophyllia,* &c.) as the variously modified direct descendants of individuals which were once fully developed, though organically connected together. On the other hand we have the view especially urged by HUXLEY and METSCHNIKOFF, that these parts are only organs which never existed as fully formed individuals.

At first thought it would appear tolerably clear that the zooids of *Renilla* must have acquired their present structure simply through having degenerated from individuals resembling the sexual polyps. They agree closely with the latter in general structure, the differences consisting for the most part in the absence of organs

---

* " Revision of the Polyps of the Eastern Coast of the United States," Bull. Mus. Comp. Zool., Cambridge : 1864.

like the tentacles or mesenterial filaments, which could be of no use as the polyp gradually became exclusively adapted to the performance of a single function (taking in or discharging water). There are some structural details in the rudimentary zooid which seem scarcely explicable if not due to direct inheritance from a fully developed polyp. Such characters are the absence of a calyx-tooth from the ventral chamber and the presence of two long calyx-teeth on the ventro-lateral chambers. In some of the Pennatulids, according to KÖLLIKER, the zooids even possess a pair of mesenterial filaments on the two dorsal septa, and the presence of such rudimentary organs in the zooids would seem to be a strong indication of their descent by degeneration from sexual polyps.

A moment's consideration shows however an insurmountable difficulty in the way of this view. The zooids are far too numerous to have ever been represented by full-sized polyps, for there would not have been room for them on the colony. The dorsal zooids on a single polyp number from 20 to 70 or more in different species of *Renilla*, and it is obvious that even a far smaller number of full-sized polyps could not possibly have stood upon the dorsal side of a single individual. The same difficulty exists in many other Pennatulids, as in *Veretillum* or in some species of *Pennatula* (e.g., *P. rubra*), where almost the entire ventral surface is covered with closely set zooids.

Hence the sexual polyps and the zooids cannot be regarded as equivalent members of the community, for they are not divergent modifications of identical ancestral forms. The zooids are new formations, acquired after the rest of the colony was established. In this case the question as to the "individuality" of the zooid is merely a verbal one; for if descent be made the criterion we cannot consider them such, and yet they are absolutely indistinguishable from young polyps. The interesting point is that buds may appear in a colony which never attain full development as ordinary individuals but are arrested at an early stage, before they have acquired all of their organs, and made to play a part in the physiological division of labour. If polymorphism thus produced may occur in the Pennatulid community, there is no reason why it may not occur in the Siphonophora, and it is possible that some of the members of the latter organism may have had such an origin. These members may be called "individuals" or "organs which simulate individuals," according to our fancy, the distinction being merely verbal.

Such a view would perhaps partially reconcile the conflicting views respecting the nature of Siphonophora referred to at p. 804. It is admitted by the advocates of the polymorphism theory that some of the structures of the Siphonophora—as, for instance, the tentacles—are not to be regarded as modified individuals ("Persons" of HAECKEL) but are simply organs belonging to the true individuals, though they cannot be distinguished from the latter by their ontogenetic development. It is not improbable that other members of the organism—for instance, the hydrophyllia or pneumatocysts — may have the significance of imperfectly developed buds which owe their origin not to degeneration from more highly organised individuals but to arrest of development at an early age. The possibility still remains that some other members—for instance, the feeding polyps or the nectocalyces — may be the direct descendants of fully-developed functional individuals which have become adapted to different functions in the physiological division of labour.

The possibility must be borne in mind that the various members of a compound organism are not necessarily of morphological equivalence — which is simply a convenient term to denote identity of ancestral origin—and that, according as the members are or are not equivalent, different forms of polymorphism are to be distinguished. In some cases, as among some Hydroida, the polymorphism seems clearly the result of a physiological division of labour among members which were originally completely and similarly developed as individuals. Such communities alone can be regarded as polymorphic in the sense in which this term was originally applied by LEUCKART to the Siphonophora. The polymorphism of *Renilla* and other Penna-tulid colonies has probably had in part a different origin and such cases must be clearly distinguished from typical polymorphism. For example, in some Pennatulids two distinct forms of secondary polyps may be recognised, viz. : feeding polyps possessing tentacles and sexual polyps destitute of tentacles. These two forms are probably to be regarded as differently modified descendants of sexual polyps like those of *Renilla*, in which the functions of nutrition and reproduction were united. To this extent the colony is therefore polymorphic in the ordinary sense. The remaining members of the community, viz. : the zooids, have however, probably had a different origin, since they are buds which never attain to complete development and never did so in the past.

The zooid is in every respect—physiological as well as anatomical—identical with the young bud which is destined to form a sexual polyp. Moreover the zooid may in some Pennatulids under some circumstances actually develop into a polyp, as KÖLLIKER states, and I have myself observed. The zooid is to be regarded therefore as a bud in a state of arrested development, which has however acquired the power of asexual multiplication.

We must therefore consider the difficult question as to the agency which originally caused the arrest of development in the buds. How, it may be asked, can in the first place a bud have been produced identical in all respects with the buds which are to form mature polyps, and yet incapable of full development ?

It is perhaps impossible to give a complete answer to this question, but the key to the solution of the problem lies possibly in the fact that the zooid, although in an embryonic state, possesses nevertheless the power of asexual multiplication. As pointed out on a preceding page, the secondary zooids of a group are to be regarded as offspring of the primary zooid and not directly of the sexual polyp on which they are placed. We may therefore explain their rudimentary structure as the result of inheritance from the primary zooid, and hence have only to consider how the latter can have been produced.

It has already been stated that the primary zooid is almost always larger and more perfectly developed than the secondary zooids derived from it. If, then, the secondary zooid owes its rudimentary structure to inheritance from a slightly more advanced bud, may not the primary zooid, as Dr. W. K. BROOKS has suggested to me, have been produced by the multiplication of a still more perfect bud, like the zooid, for instance, of *Halisceptrum* which possesses a pair of mesenterial filaments? This in turn may have been formed by the multiplication of a more highly organised bud, and so on until a fully developed polyp stood at the beginning of the series. This will be rendered more clear by an illustration, in the consideration of which it is necessary to bear clearly in mind the fact that the immature bud of the sexual polyp performs the same function as the zooid and that this function is of vital importance to the organism.

Suppose a secondary bud, A, to give rise by asexual multiplication to a tertiary bud, B, which remained longer in a rudimentary state and developed less perfectly than A, and hence performed more perfectly the function of taking in water. In a succeeding generation B gives rise to still more rudimentary individuals, C, and so on through many generations until true zooids, permanently rudimentary, were produced. The functions of the rudimentary and of the fully developed individuals being entirely different, the interme iate or transitional forms would perform both functions less perfectly. They would therefore tend to disappear by natural selection until a colony would result like *Renilla* in which no well-marked transitional forms existed. Such a process is widely different from direct degeneration since each stage of the series is not represented in the preceding stage. Thus in the foregoing illustration C is not represented in the preceding stage by B, but is an entirely new individual produced as a bud upon B; and this is true of each succeeding stage. If, then, the ancestral history of a zooid could be followed backward from one generation to another we should not find it becoming more and more highly organised, but a point would be reached when it would entirely disappear.

This view is perhaps of too speculative a nature to be accepted without reserve, but it has at least the merit of showing how structures like zooids, of considerable complexity, might suddenly arise without direct descent from or the gradual modification of any corresponding structures in a preceding generation.

In regard to the nature of such structures as the zooids, HUXLEY's definition of the "organs" of the Hydrozoa appears to me most satisfactory. They are, namely :— "Organs which tend more or less completely to become independent existences or zooids." (The term zooid is here used in a general sense and not in the special sense employed in this paper.) A careful distinction must, however, be drawn between these "organs" and those which are due to the direct degeneration or other modification of complete individuals; and the possibility must be borne in mind that these different kinds of structures may co-exist in the so-called polymorphic communities.

Beaufort, N.C., August 1, 1882.

[*Appendix.*—During the passage of this paper through the press, I have discovered in several genera of Alcyonaria that the dorsal filaments are, in fact, ectodermic downgrowths from the stomodœum, whereas the six others are strictly entodermic structures. My failure to recognise this fundamental difference was due to the circumstance that the entodermic filaments become at an early stage perfectly continuous with the stomodœal ectoderm, like the dorsal filaments, and my most favourable sections happened to be in every case through the entodermic filaments. For a description of these new observations I must refer to a forthcoming paper in the 'Mittheilungen aus der Zoologischen Station zu Neapel.'—Naples, September 20, 1883.]

Explanation of Figures.

The following lettering is used uniformly in all the figures. Other reference letters are explained for the separate figures. The figures of sections are with a few exceptions drawn with the camera. Those of the segmenting eggs and of the external appearances of the colony are free-hand.

al. Gastric cavity.

a.c. Axial cells of peduncular septum.

c. Central cells.

c.m. Circular muscles.

ch. Radial chamber.

c.c. Calyx-teeth.

d.c.x. Dorsal calyx-tooth.

d.l.ch. Dorso-lateral chamber.

d.l.f. Dorso-lateral mesenterial filaments.

d.l.s. Dorso-lateral septa.

d.s. Dorsal septa.

d.f. Dorsal mesenterial filaments.

e. Free edge of peduncular septum.

ec. Ectoderm.

en. Entoderm.

e.z. Exhalent zooid.

f. Mesenterial filament.

l.m. Longitudinal muscles.

œ. Œsophagus.

p¹., p²., p³., &c. Sexual polyps, or buds destined to become such, numbered in the order of their appearance.

ped. Peduncle.

p.s.   Peduncular septum.
s.   Septa.
s.l.   Supporting lamella.
sp.   Spicule or spicule cell.
st.   Stomodœum.
t.   Tentacle.
v.   Ventral chamber or ventral side.
r.s.   Ventral septa.
v.cx.   Ventral (ventro-lateral) calyx-teeth.
v.f.   Ventral mesenterial filaments.
r.l.s.   Ventro-lateral septa.
v.l.f.   Ventro-lateral mesenterial filaments.
r.l.ch.   Ventro-lateral chamber.
y.   Yolk.
z.   Inhalent zooids.

PLATE 52.

Figs. 1 to 14. Segmentation of an egg which divides at first into eight spheres. Time as follows :—Fig. 1, 8.50 A.M. ; 2, one minute ; 3, two m.; 4, seven m.; 5, ten m.; 6, twenty-five m.; 7, thirty-four m.; 8, fifty-five m.; 9, sixty-three m.; 10, sixty-eight m.; 11, seventy-five m.; 12, ninety m.; 13, ninety-eight m.; 14, one hundred and fifteen m. × 85.

Figs. 15 to 18. Continuation of segmentation, from another specimen. Time as follows :—Fig. 15, 10 A.M.; 16, ten m.; 17, twenty-seven m.; 18, thirty-two m. × 85.

Figs. 19 to 24. Unusual mode of segmentation. Time as follows :—Fig. 19, 7.55 A.M.; 20, two m.; 21, ten m.; 22, twenty m.; 23, twenty-three m.; 24, forty m. × 65.

Figs. 25 to 27. Division of an egg into two spheres. × 65.

Figs. 28, 29. Egg divided into four spheres. × 65.

PLATE 53.

Figs. 30 to 37. Segmentation of an egg which divided at once into sixteen spheres. Time not recorded. × 65.

Figs. 38 to 41. Unequal segmentation beginning with sixteen spheres. Time as follows :—Fig. 38, 9.7 A.M.; 39, same in different position ; 40, thirty-three m.; 41, thirty-six m. × 65.

Figs. 42 to 44. Another specimen illustrating unequal segmentation beginning with sixteen spheres. Time :—Fig. 42, 9.20 A.M.; 43, same in different position ; 44, thirty m. × 65.

Figs. 45 to 48. Segmentation of an egg which first divided incompletely into eight spheres, and afterwards completely into sixteen. Time :—Fig. 45, 9.5 A.M.; 46, five m.; 47, twenty-one m.; 48, thirty-three m. × 65.

Figs. 49 to 58. Segmentation of an egg which first divided irregularly and incompletely into eight. The sphere marked *a* failed to divide with the others at the third cleavage but divided at the fourth (57). Time :—Fig. 49, 10.29 A.M.; 50, four m.; 51, six m.; 52, fifteen m.; 53, different position, seventeen m.; 54, thirty-one m.; 55, forty-one m.; 56, forty-eight m.; 57, fifty-six m.; 58, sixty-eight m. × 65.

Figs. 59 to 62. "Partial" or progressive form of segmentation. Time :—Fig. 59, 10.6 A.M.; 60, eight m.; 61, nineteen m.; 62, same in different position. × 65.

Figs. 63 to 67. Segmentation similar to the last. Time :—Fig. 63, 11.35 A.M.; 64, nine m.; 65, thirteen m.; 66, nineteen m.; 67, twenty-one m. × 65.

PLATE 54.

Figs. 68 to 72. Very unequal and irregular form of segmentation. Time :—Not recorded. × 65.

Figs. 73 to 76. Segmentation of *Leptogorgia*. Time :—Fig. 73, 10.14 A.M.; 74, three m.; 75, twenty-one m.; 76, thirty-six m. × 70.

Figs. 77 to 85. Further segmentation of *Leptogorgia* ; another specimen. Time :— Fig. 77, 10.5 A.M.; 78, fifteen m.; 79, twenty-four m.; 80, thirty-five m.; 81, seventy-eight m.; 82, ninety-five m.; 83, one h. fifty-five m.; 84, two h. five m.; 85, two h. twenty-five m. × 70.

Fig. 86. Section through unfertilised egg showing germinal vesicle and spot, *d*. × 85.

Fig. 87. Section through egg immediately before segmentation. × 85.

Fig. 88. Section through the same egg, separated from the last section by three intervening ones. × 85.

Fig. 89. Section through an egg in the act of division into sixteen spheres, directly from the unfertilised egg. × 85.

Fig. 90. Section through an egg which from the exterior appeared to consist of eight spheres. × 85.

Fig. 91. Section through an egg with sixteen superficial spheres and a central unsegmented mass. × 85.

Fig. 92. Similar to the last but with the central mass much reduced. × 85.

Fig. 93. The spheres now extend to the centre of the egg and the central mass has nearly vanished. × 85.

Fig. 94. Blastula, with distinct segmentation cavity.   One of the spheres, *a*, is apparently undergoing a delamination cleavage.   × 85.

Fig. 95. Egg in resting stage with unsegmented central mass.   × 190.

PLATE 55.

Fig. 96. In this embryo the inner ends of the spheres are separating or have just separated from the outer portion.   × 190.

Fig. 97. Delamination completed.   × 145.

Fig. 98. Unsegmented egg or one in the act of division.   To show vertical amphiasters.   × 85.

Fig. 99. Section through an egg in which the delamination is partially accomplished but is in progress in the cells *a* and *b*.   The section is incomplete below but complete above.   × 85.

Fig. 100. Later stage; the last to show delamination still in progress.   The section is complete above and below but incomplete on the sides.   × 85.

Figs. 100*a*., 100*b*., 100*c*. Three larvæ of about twelve hours to show irregularity in form.   × 65.

Fig. 101. Free-swimming larva of about twenty-four hours.   × 45.

Fig. 102. A slightly older larva under compression, showing septa.   The ventro-lateral septa could not be followed up to the peduncular septum as it ordinarily can.   × 45.

Fig. 103. Larva of about three and a-half days' showing septa and buds. Dorsal view.   × 45.

Fig. 104. The same larva, from left side.   × 45.

Fig. 105. Same specimen shown in figs. 103 and 104 in a state of strong contraction.   × 45.

Fig. 106. *Leptogorgia*. Same embryo shown in figs. 77 to 85, ten minutes later than fig. 85.   × 70.

Fig. 107. Another specimen two hours later in the irregular stage.   × 70.

Fig. 108. The same specimen twenty hours later.   × 70.

Fig. 109. *Leptogorgia* two days old.   × 70.

PLATE 56.

Fig. 110. The same, three days.   × 110.

Fig. 111. The same as last under compression showing ectoderm and stomodæum, *st*.   × 110.

Fig. 112. The same, four days old.   × 110.

Fig. 113. The same, eight days; recently attached to bottom.   × 50.

Fig. 114. Two larvæ united together.   × 50.

Fig. 115. The same, eleven days. At *a* is the posterior thickened region which secretes the axis. × 50.

Fig. 116. The same individual, twelve days. × 50.

Fig. 116*ª*. Part of wall of body more highly magnified to show spicules in ectoderm.

Fig. 117. The same, thirteen days. Mesenterial filaments well developed. × 50.

Fig. 118. Section through *Leptogorgia* embryo of six hours. × 160.

Fig. 120. Section through *Renilla* embryo of about four hours. × 290.

PLATE 57.

Fig. 119. Section through *Renilla* embryo of four and three-quarter hours.

Fig. 121. Section through an embryo of eight and a-half hours. × 290.

Fig. 122. Portion of a section of same stage more highly magnified. × 880.

Fig. 123. Same as last. × 880.

Fig. 124. Yolk cells from last with deutoplasm spherules. × 880.

Fig. 125. Longitudinal section through embryo of twenty-two and a-half hours. × 195.

PLATE 58.

Fig. 126. Portion of same more highly magnified. × 350.

Fig. 127. Part of a section through a twenty-five-hours' embryo. × 350.

Fig. 128. Longitudinal section through a twenty-nine-hours' embryo. × 165.

Fig. 129. Part of the same more highly magnified. × 350.

Fig. 130. Part of section through a fifty-two-hours' larva. × 350.

Fig. 131. Part of section of a twenty-eight-hours' embryo to show proliferation of ectoderm. × 350.

Fig. 132. Part of section through an embryo further advanced than the last to show formation of supporting lamella; *a* represents a single ectoderm cell with swollen base, *b*; *b b* are the rounded bodies which have separated from the ectoderm cells; *c* is one of the rounded cells from the deeper parts of the ectoderm. × 350.

Fig. 133. Part of longitudinal section through a twenty-six-hours' embryo to show formation of supporting lamella.

Fig. 134. Longitudinal section through a forty-hours' larva to show formation of stomodæum. × 230.

PLATE 59.

Fig. 135. Longitudinal section through a forty-eight-hours' larva. × 230.

Fig. 136. Vertical longitudinal section through a fifty-two-hours' larva. × 165.

Fig. 137. Longitudinal section through a seventy-five-hours' larva. Œsophagus still closed. × 140.

Fig. 138. Similar section through a slightly later stage (100 hours). × 140.

Fig. 139. A similar section of a sixty-two-hours' embryo; the œsophagus has just broken through. × 140.

Fig. 140. Longitudinal section of seventy-five-hours' larva. Mouth fully formed, but "œsophageal plug" (*pl.*) still adhering to the edge of one of the septa. × 140.

Fig. 141. Sixty-hours' larva. Mouth breaking through bottom of stomodæum. × 140.

Fig. 142. Transverse section through anterior part of forty-eight-hours' larva. × 315.

PLATE 60.

Fig. 143. Transverse section from same specimen further back at the level of lower end of œsophagus. × 315.

Fig. 144. Transverse section through anterior part of a four-days' larva. × 315.

Fig. 145. From same larva at lower end of œsophagus. × 315.

Fig. 146. Transverse section of four-days' larva posterior to œsophagus. × 350.

Fig. 147. Part of a transverse section through a forty-eight-hours' larva showing a septum and general histology. × 660.

Fig. 147*ª*. Portion of ectoderm from last. × 880.

PLATE 61.

Fig. 148. Section through lateral attachment of peduncular septum to body-wall. Forty-eight hours. × 350.

Fig. 149. Section through radial septum and part of body-wall. Forty-eight hours. × 350.

Fig. 150. Longitudinal section through posterior part of body of a forty-hours' larva to show formation of peduncular septum. × 135.

Fig. 151. Transverse section through posterior part of a forty-eight-hours' larva showing peduncular septum. × 315.

Fig. 152. Transverse section through the free-edge of the peduncular septum. Forty-eight hours. × 180.

Fig. 153. Part of longitudinal section through peduncular septum, highly magnified, to show axial cells. × 350.

Fig. 154. Transverse section in front of peduncular septum. Forty-eight hours. × 315.

Fig. 155. Longitudinal section just above peduncular septum. × 220.

Fig. 156. Transverse section through peduncular septum at its attachment to the body-wall. Forty-five hours.

PLATE 62.

Figs. 157, 158, 159. Longitudinal sections through 100-hours' larvæ showing continuity of stomodæal ectoderm with the mesenterial filaments. ×140.

Figs. 160, 161. Surface views of four-days' larvæ to show muscular fibres. ×880.

Fig. 162. Transverse section through the dorsal median tract of longitudinal muscles. Four days. ×880.

Fig. 163. Transverse section through ventral median tract of longitudinal muscles. ×880.

Fig. 164. Corresponding section through a younger specimen. ×880.

Fig. 165. Transverse section through septum and a septal tract of longitudinal muscles. ×880.

PLATE 63.

Fig. 166. Transverse section through septal tract below the septum.

Fig. 167. Transverse section through body-wall and peduncular septum to show longitudinal muscles in the ventral side of the latter.

Fig. 168. Part of longitudinal section through the body-wall showing the circular muscles. ×880.

Fig. 169. Transverse section through body-wall showing circular muscles in longitudinal section. ×880.

Fig. 170. Various forms of myoblasts from the entoderm. ×700.

Fig. 171. Cells from the deeper layers of the ectoderm with spicules developing in their interior. ×700.

Fig. 172. Entoderm cells with spicules in course of formation. ×700.

PLATE 64.

Fig. 173. Section through a four-days' larva passing through one of the buds (p^1.). ×315.

Fig. 174. Similar section passing through bud at p^1.; a, lateral forward extension of peduncular septum. ×315.

Fig. 175. Transverse section through four-days' larva passing through both buds. ×315.

Fig. 176. Ventral view of four-and-a-half-days' young polyp. ×56.

Fig. 177. The same specimen one day later from the left side. ×56.

PLATE 65.

Fig. 178. Young polyp of about nine days from right side. ×30.

Fig. 178^a. Tentacle. ×45.

Fig. 178^b. Bud in profile view.   × 90.
Fig. 178^c. Bud from above.   × 90.
Fig. 179. Right lateral view of part of a somewhat older polyp.   × 45.
Fig. 180. Dorsal view of last.   × 45.
Fig. 181. Dorsal view of polyp with recently developed exhalent zooid.   × 30.
Fig. 182. Dorso-lateral view of polyp with two pairs of buds.   × 30.
Fig. 183. Lateral view of polyp with third pair of buds just appearing.   × 40.
Fig. 183^a. Dorsal view of peduncle partly contracted to show bands of circular muscles.
Fig. 183^b. Upper view of bud p^3.
Fig. 183^c. Same bud in lateral optical section.
Fig. 184. Ventral view of part of polyp with three pairs of buds.   × 40.
Fig. 184^a. Oral view of p^1.

PLATE 66.

Fig. 185. Dorsal view of young colony having five pairs of buds and three zooids.
   × 40.
Fig. 186. Dorsal view of part of young colony with seven pairs of lateral buds and three pairs of zooids.   × 60.
Fig. 187. Dorsal view of fully expanded colony with twelve pairs of lateral buds and numerous zooids.   × 30.
Fig. 188. Dorsal view of colony in a state of contraction with thirteen pairs of lateral buds.   × 30.
Fig. 189. Dorsal view of left half of the disc of a young colony. The zooids have multiplied to form groups represented by small circles.   × 15.

PLATE 67.

Figs. 190 to 193. Series illustrating development of calyx-teeth. From a mature colony.   × 20.
Figs. 194 to 203. Series illustrating the multiplication of a single primary zooid (p.) to a group of eighteen.   × 80.
Fig. 204. Ventral view in optical section of the bases of the first two pairs of lateral buds to show the partition between them and its free-edge ($fl.$) below.   × 50.
Fig. 205. Ventral view in optical section of an older colony to show further development of the lateral folds ($fl.$).   × 50.
Fig. 206. Similar view of a still older specimen in which the two folds have met to form a single fold beneath the peduncular septum.   × 50.
Fig. 207. Similar view of older specimen in which the closure of the ventral canal is well advanced   × 50.

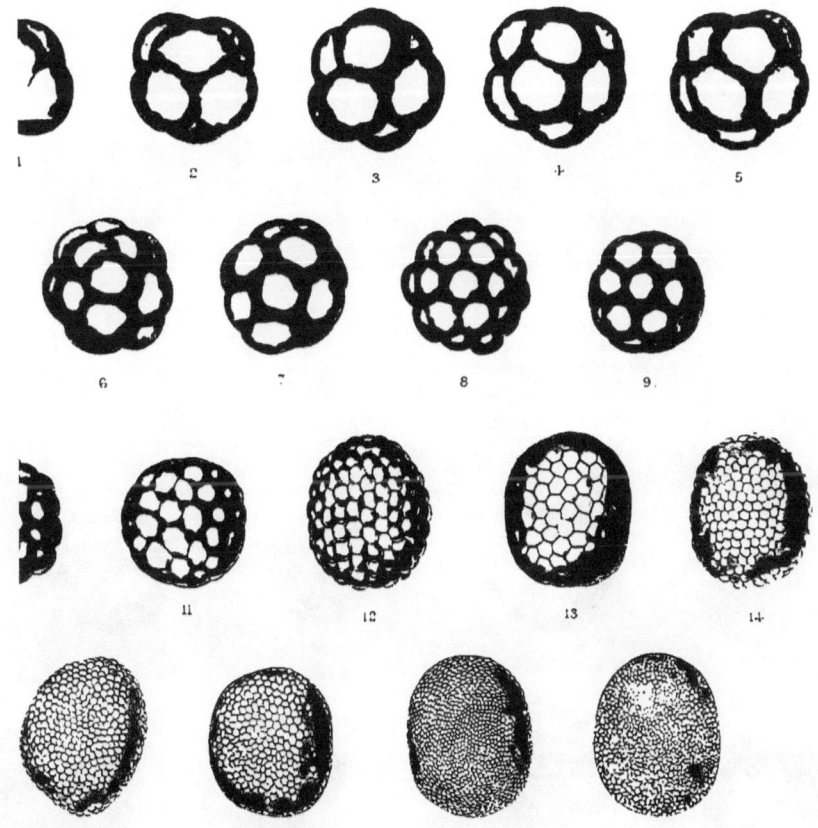

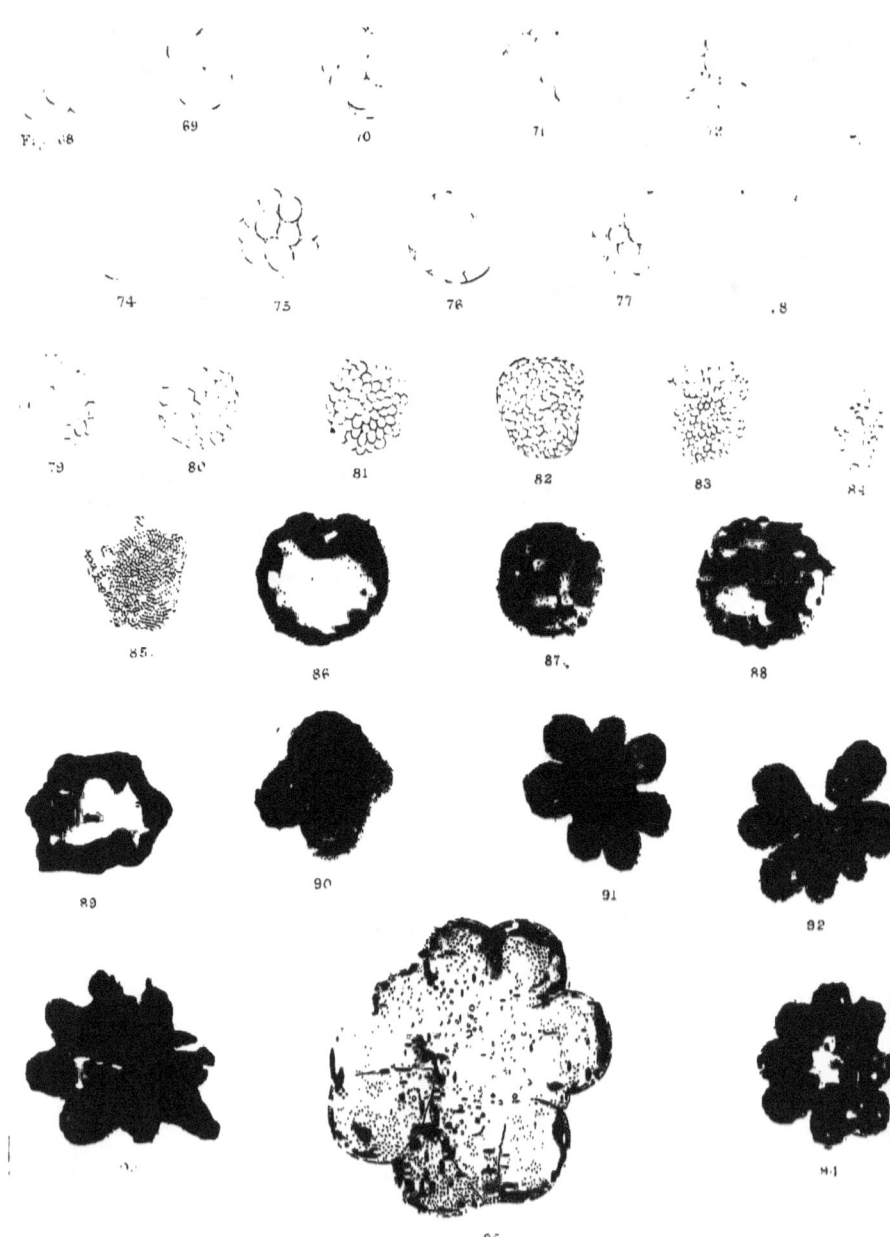

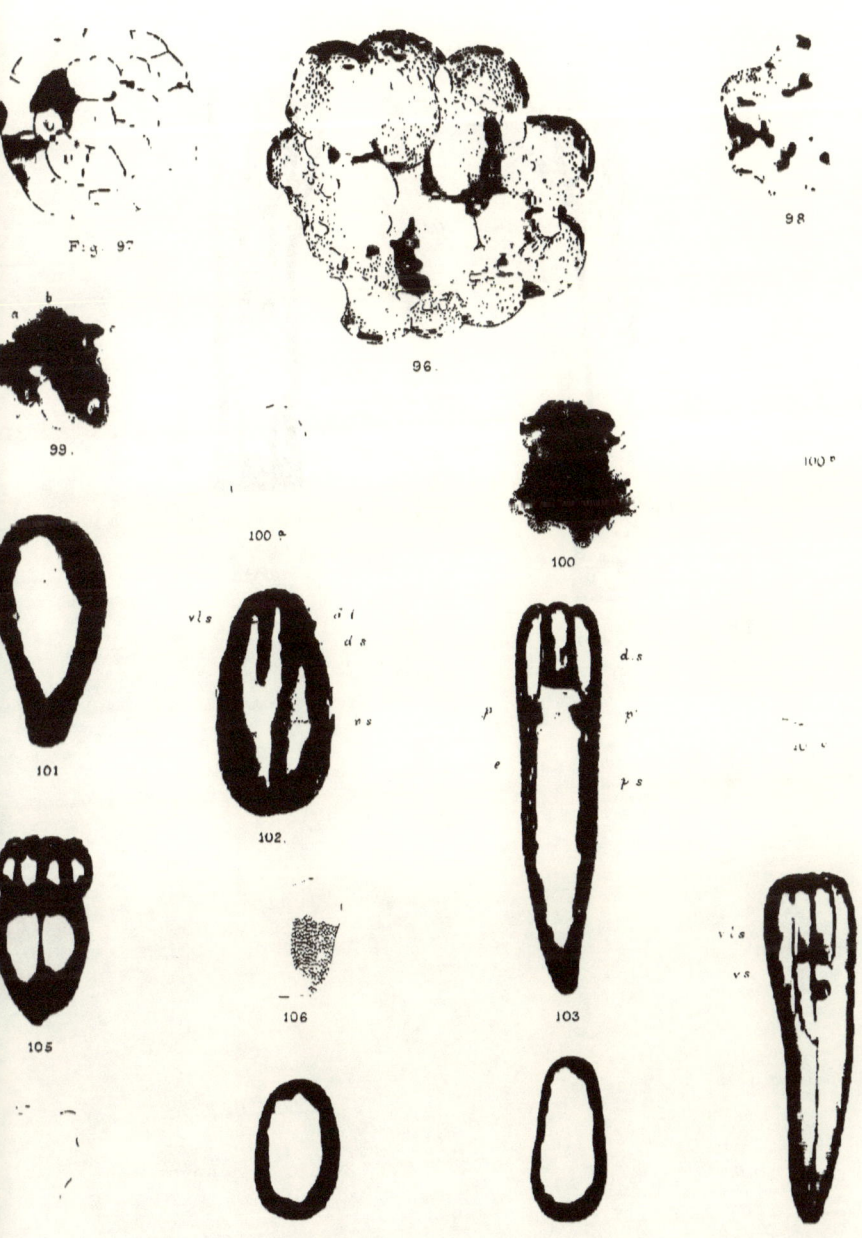

Fig. 97

96.

98

99.

100 e

100

100 e

101

102.

vls d.l
d.s

v.s

p

e

d.s

p

v.s

10 c

105

106

103

v.s
v.s

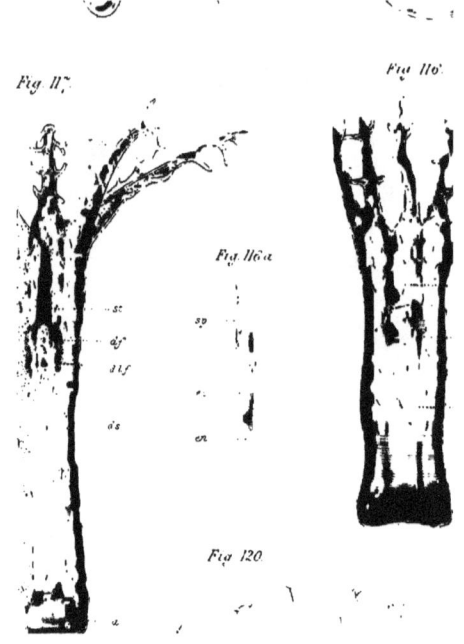

Fig. 117.

Fig. 119.

Fig. 118 a

Fig. 120

Phil. Trans. 1883. *Plate* 57.

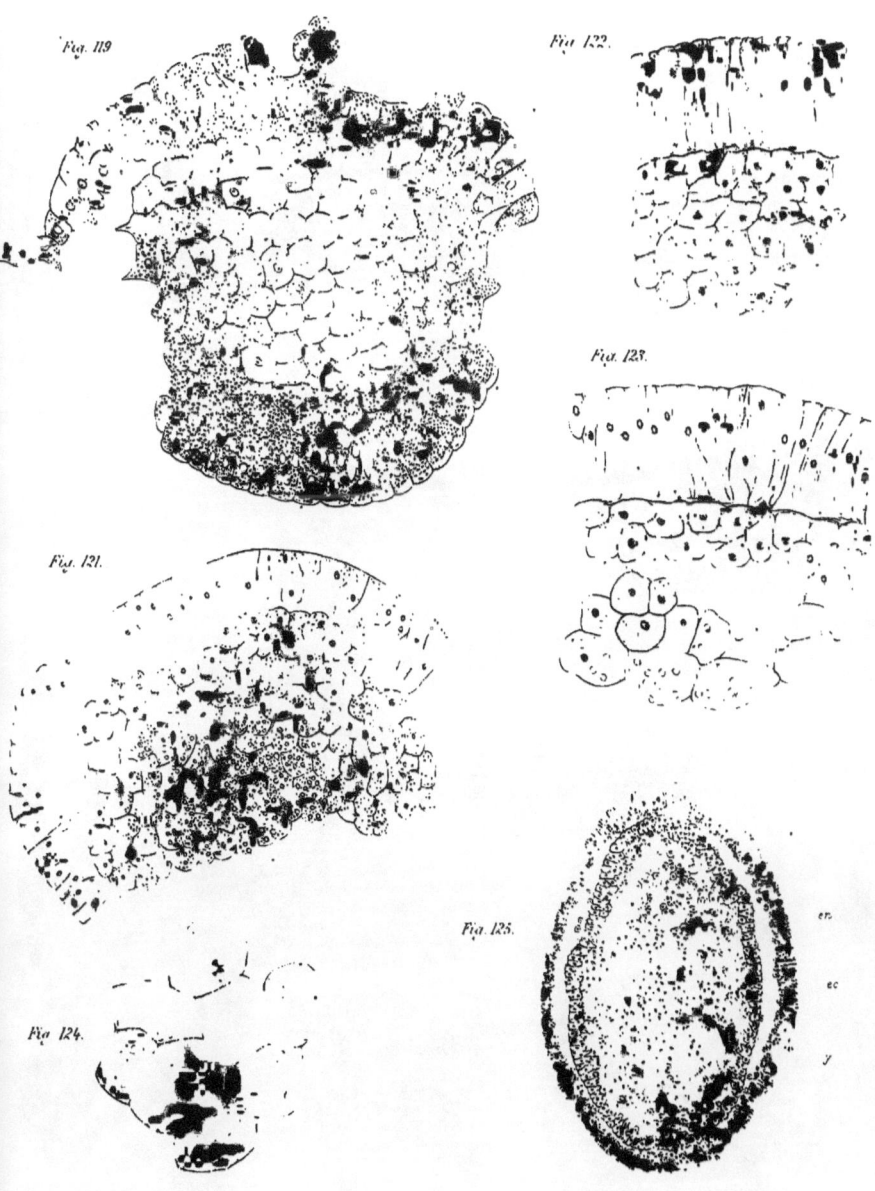

Fig. 119

Fig. 122.

Fig. 123.

Fig. 121.

Fig. 125.

Fig. 124.

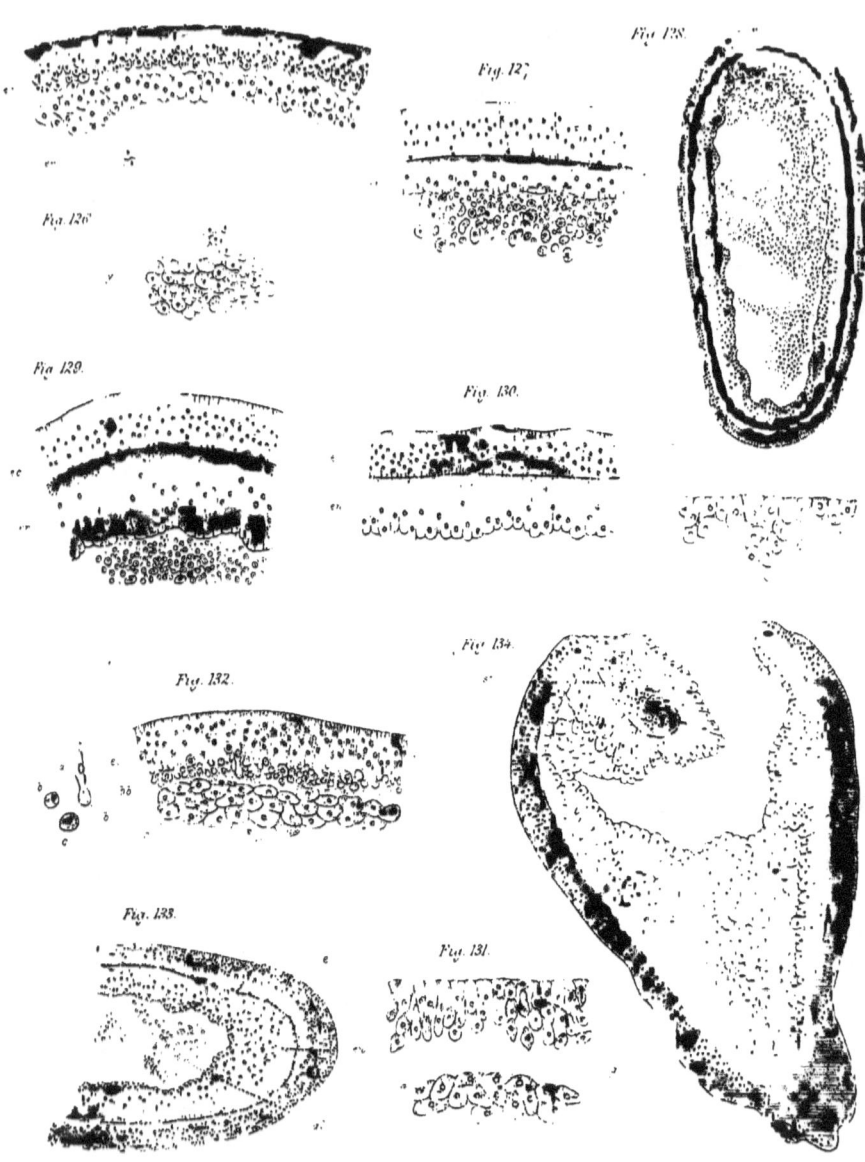

Fig. 126.

Fig. 127.

Fig. 128.

Fig. 129.

Fig. 130.

Fig. 132.

Fig. 134.

Fig. 133.

Fig. 131.

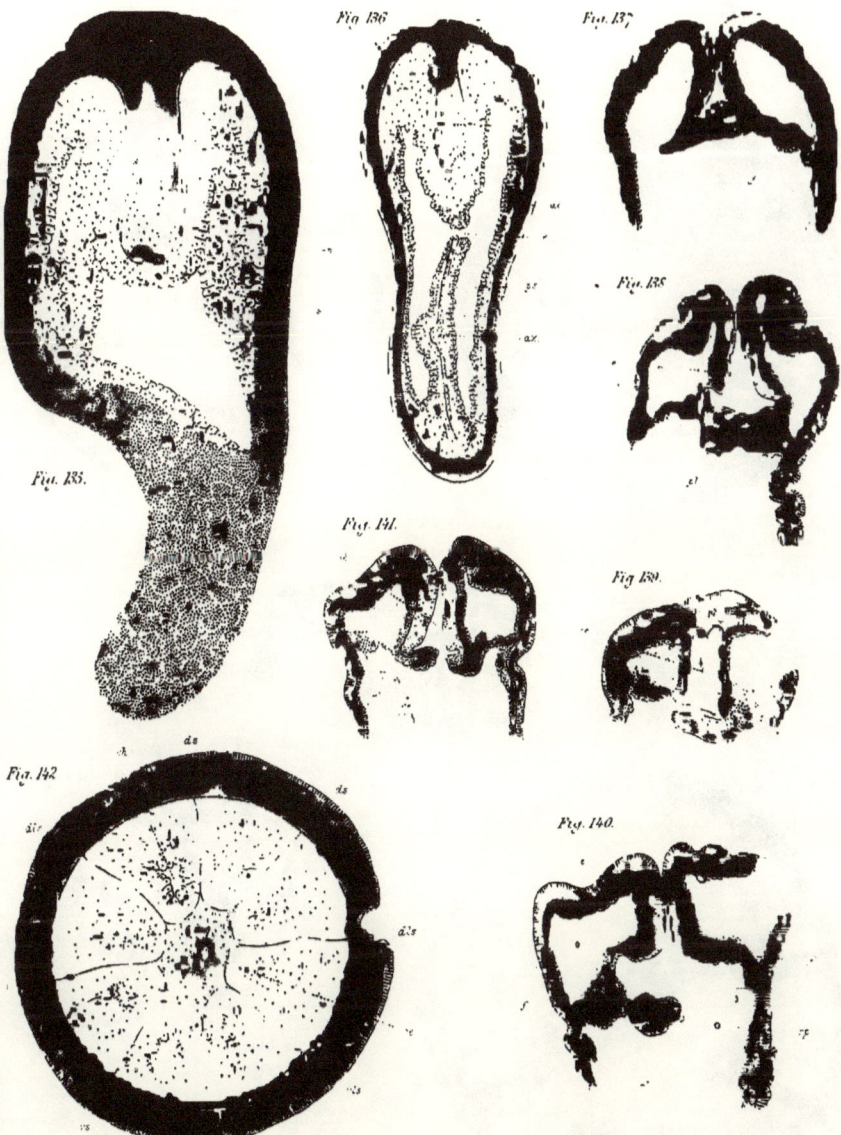

Fig. 136.

Fig. 137.

Fig. 135.

Fig. 138.

Fig. 141.

Fig. 139.

Fig. 142.

Fig. 140.

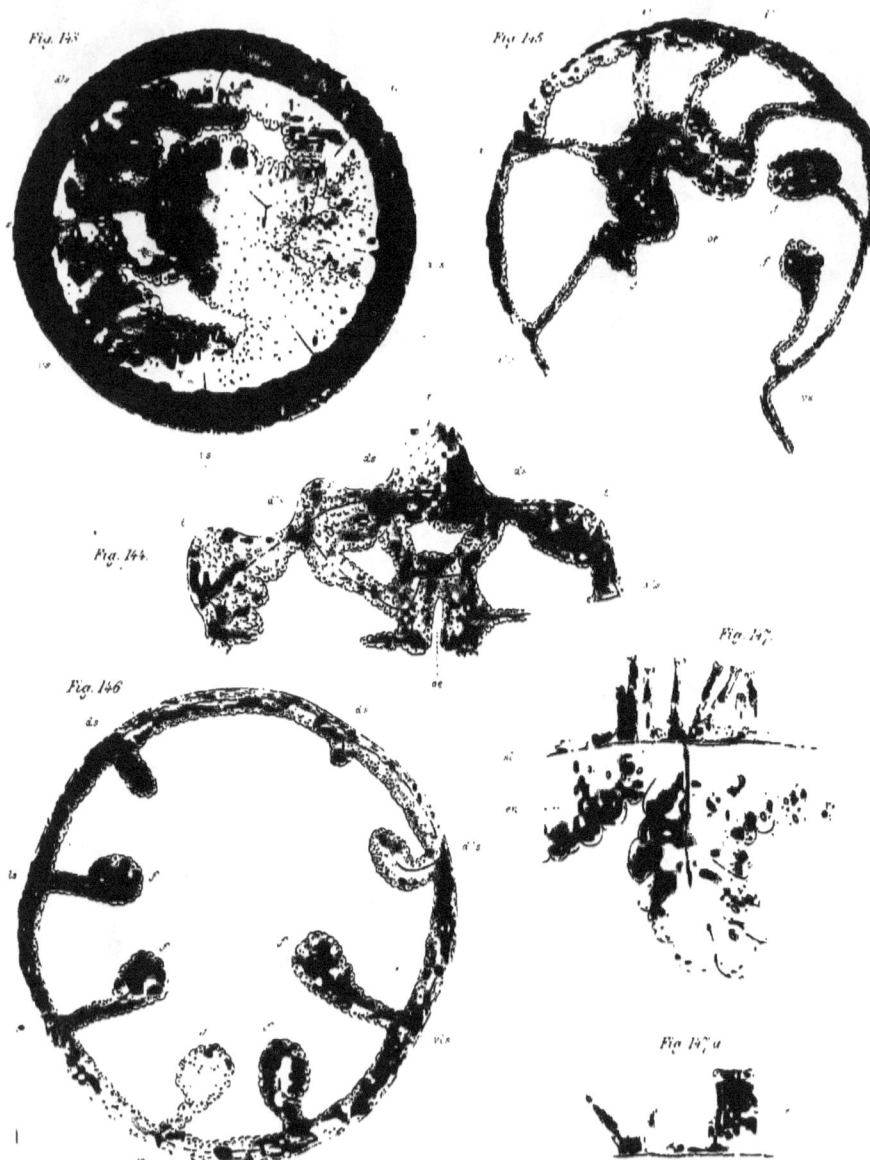

Fig. 143.

Fig. 145.

Fig. 144.

Fig. 146.

Fig. 147.

Fig. 147 a

Phil. Trans. 1883. Plate 61.

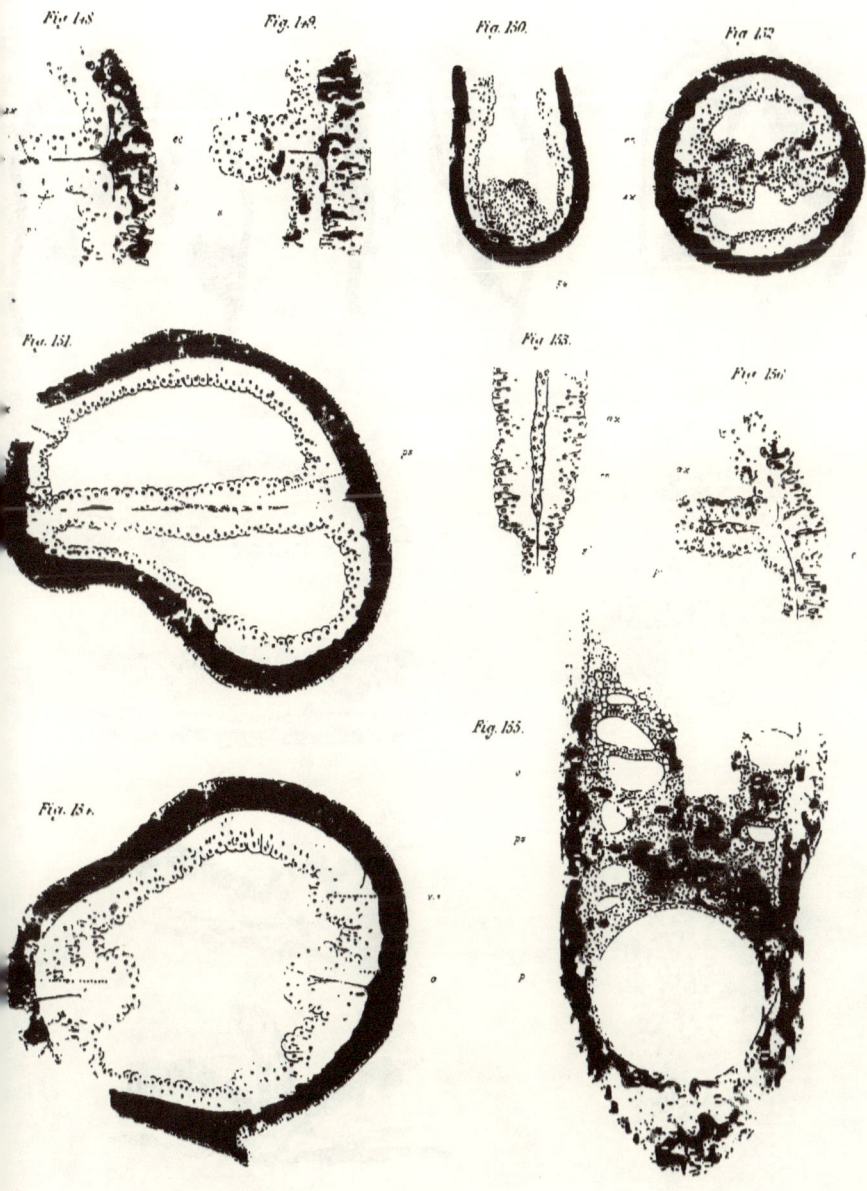

Fig. 148.

Fig. 149.

Fig. 150.

Fig. 152.

Fig. 151.

Fig. 153.

Fig. 156.

Fig. 154.

Fig. 155.

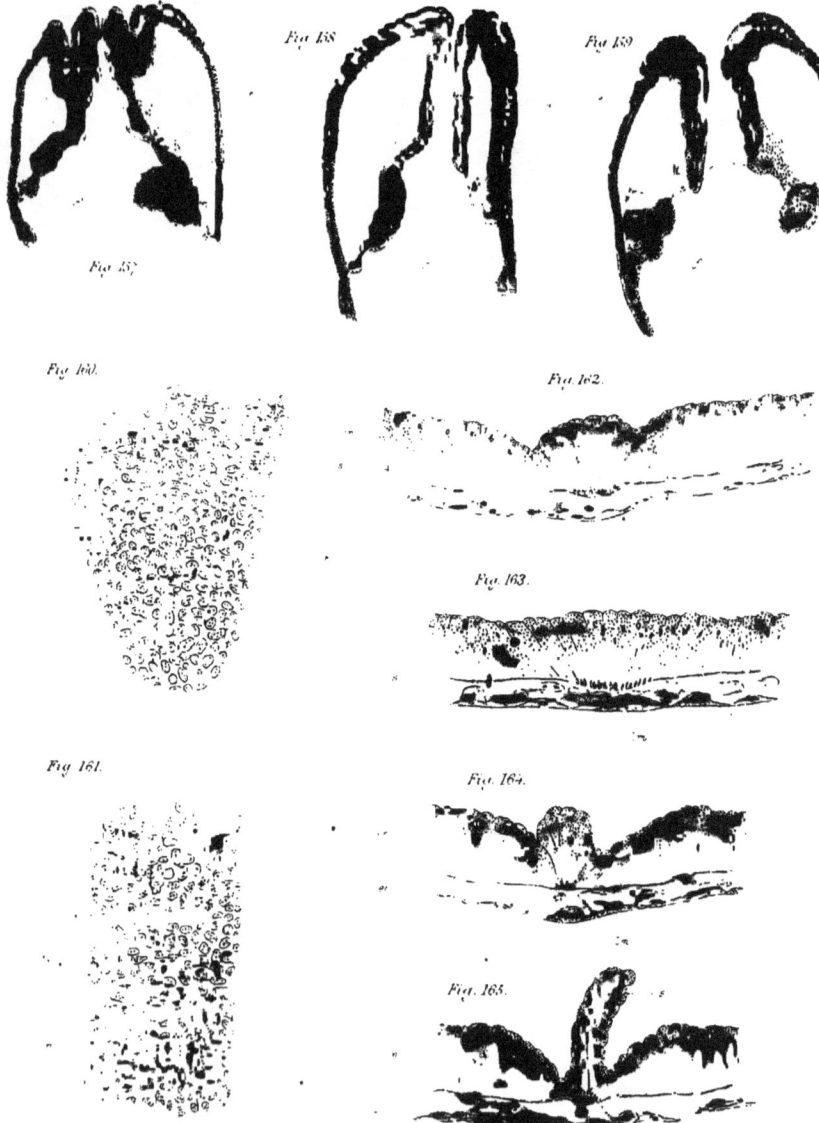

Fig. 158.

Fig. 159.

Fig. 157.

Fig. 160.

Fig. 162.

Fig. 163.

Fig. 161.

Fig. 164.

Fig. 165.

Phil. Trans 1883. Plate 63.

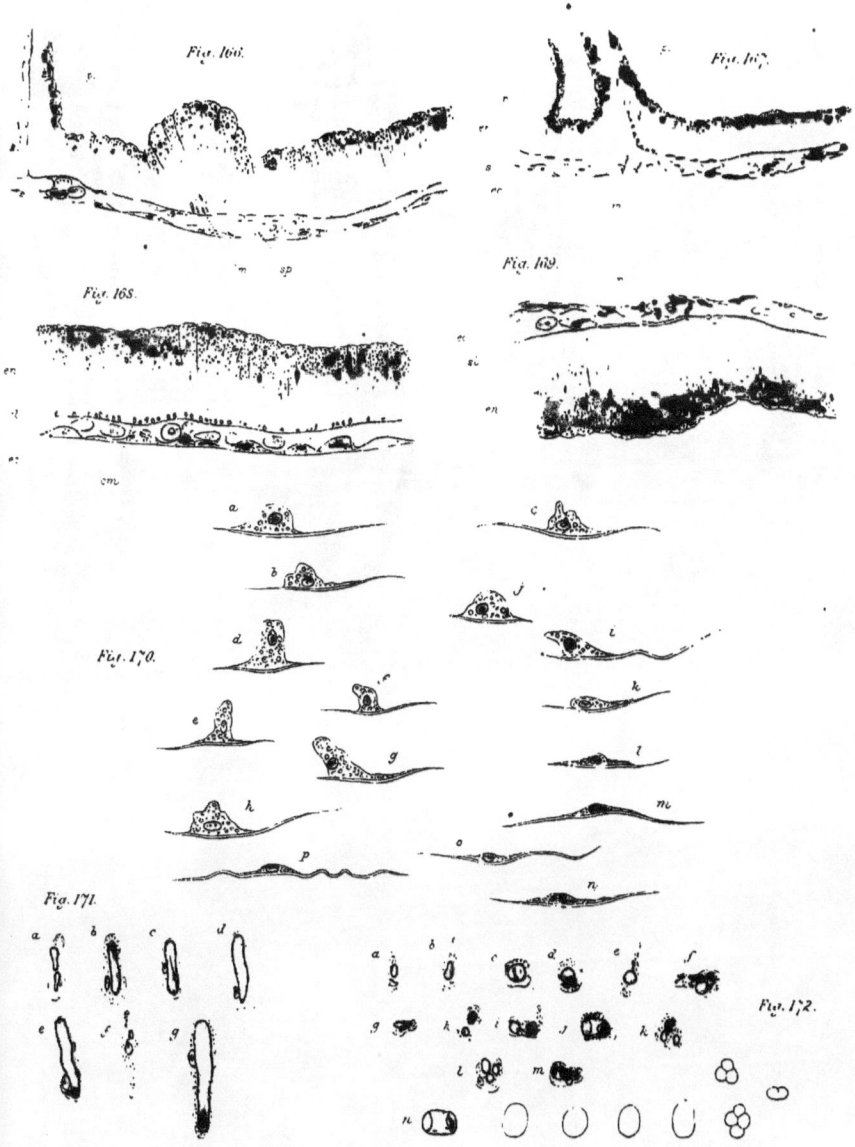

Fig. 166.

Fig. 167.

Fig. 168.

Fig. 169.

Fig. 170.

Fig. 171.

Fig. 172.

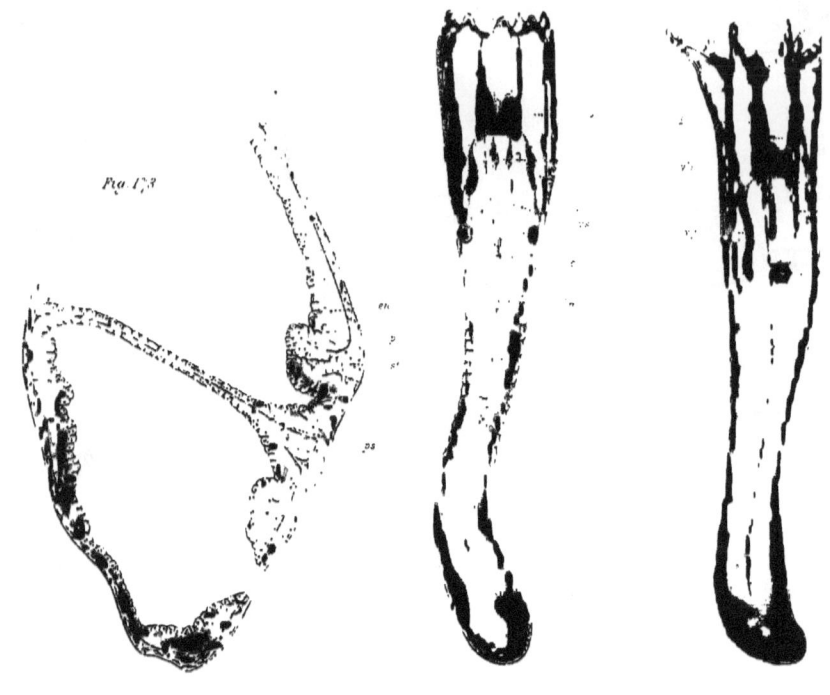

Fig. 173

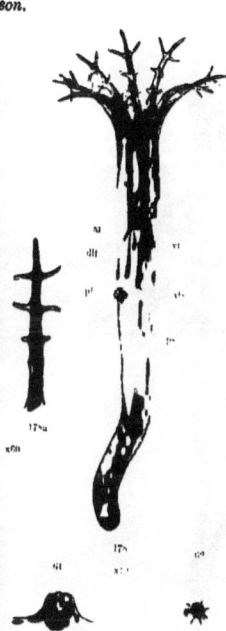

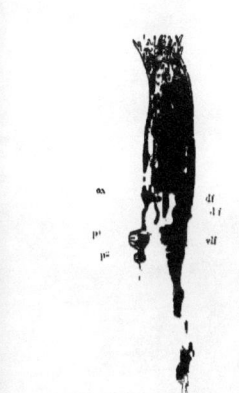
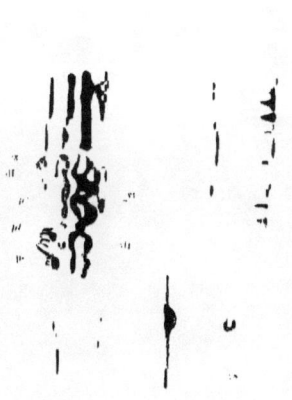
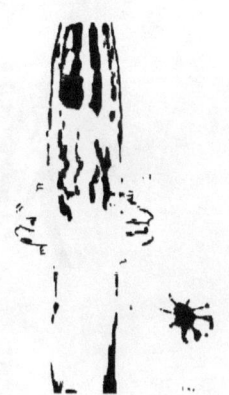

www.ingramcontent.com/pod-product-compliance
Lightning Source LLC
Chambersburg PA
CBHW020804020726
47495CB00008B/2590